P9-BZO-802

Books by Pamela F. Service

Winter of Magic's Return
A Question of Destiny
When the Night Wind Howls
Tomorrow's Magic

TOMORROW'S MAGIC

TOMORROW'S MAGIC

Pamela F. Service

A Jean Karl book

Atheneum New York 1987

Atheneum
Macmillan Publishing Company
866 Third Avenue, New York, NY 10022
Collier Macmillan Canada, Inc.

Type set by Maryland Linotype, Baltimore, Maryland
Printed and bound by Fairfield Graphics, Fairfield, Pennsylvania
Designed by Suzanne Haldane
First Edition
10 9 8 7 6 5 4 3 2 1

Library of Congress Cataloging-in-Publication Data

Service, Pamela F.   Tomorrow's magic.

"A Jean Karl book."
SUMMARY: Five hundred years after the Devastation
destroys modern civilization, the young Merlin and two
friends succeed in bringing back King Arthur to a
Britain in the grip of a nuclear winter and together
they struggle to build a new and better society despite
the evil plotting of Morgan Le Fay. Sequel to "Winter
of Magic's Return."
    1. Merlin—Juvenile fiction. [1. Merlin—Fiction.
2. Arthur, King—Fiction. 3. Fantasy] I. Title.
PZ7.S4885To 1987   [Fic]   86-32123
ISBN 0-689-31320-9

To Betsy
for all those early adventures

contents

TOMORROW'S MAGIC

one

Legends Renewed

Heather missed the ball. She leaped, but it sailed over her, inches beyond her outstretched fingers. Her fleece-lined boots thumped back onto the sand, and, laughing, she turned and ran after it.

Already the ball was rolling swiftly down the damp sand toward the ocean. It slammed against a half-buried stone, bounced into the air, and came down on a jumble of dark rocks that jutted out into the water.

Heather's hood was back, and her thin light-brown braids streamed behind her in the cold breeze. They'd just bought that ball, dyed all red and blue, from a leather worker in Ravenglass. She wasn't about to let it get washed out to sea.

Skidding to a halt at the rocks, she stepped onto them cautiously. At high tide they were mostly beneath the water, and even now their water-smoothed surfaces were damp and slimy. Her boots scraped against crusted barnacles as she stepped around tidepools and slippery patches of green to make her way out to the ball.

It had landed in a pool at the very edge of the rocks. Water surged and boomed in the deep crevasse beyond, while waves regularly slapped against the rock, filling the air with a fine salty spray. Heather licked the saltiness from her lips as she reached down and scooped the ball from the cold, clear pool. Holding it high like a torch, she turned back toward her friends on the distant beach, smiling and waving triumphantly.

She could see the two standing side by side on the dry snow-flecked sand. The veiled sunlight glinted off Welly's glasses as he hopped up and down, waving. Beside him, Earl was also waving, looking tall and thin beside Welly's sturdy plumpness. Both were yelling, but Heather couldn't hear the words over the constant rumbling and crashing of the sea behind her.

They were yelling and pointing; then both started running toward her. Clutching the ball, she began walking back. It was too late. An extra-large wave burst over the rocks, engulfing her in cold, wet foam. In the hammering surge of water, her feet slipped from the slimy rocks.

Suddenly everything was dark, wet, and cold. In panic, she opened her eyes then shut them against the stinging salt water. The darkness about her surged and eddied. She couldn't tell which was the way up, the way to air. But she needed to find it—now!

Something pulled at her, but not the ocean. An arm pulling her upward. Welly's or Earl's. They'd gotten there quickly. Her head burst through into the air. Another head was bobbing beside hers. But even through the dripping hair plastered to her face, she could see that it was not one of her friends.

It was a young blond man, and despite his own bedraggled appearance, he was grinning broadly. "Excuse the familiarity, Miss, but you seemed to need a wee bit of help."

"You'll both be needing that," came a voice from the

rocks above them, "if you don't get out before the next big wave. Come on, Welly, let's haul them up."

The two boys soon dragged Heather and her rescuer onto the rocks. "Let's get back to the beach," Earl said wrapping his dry jacket around Heather while Welly offered his to the stranger. "I'll go start a fire." Picking up his walking stick from the rocks, he hurried ahead. By the time the others reached him, he had a good fire going with a few pieces of driftwood.

Heather huddled close to the flames, shivering from cold and from the fear that had suddenly caught up with her. She spoke to the stranger through chattering teeth. "I'm sorry you got soaked, but thanks for helping me. I could have been swept out to sea like. . . . Oh, the ball! Our new ball, what happened to it?"

Welly laughed. "Here," he said, producing it from behind him. "The wave carried it neatly onto the beach. You needn't have risked life and limb for it after all."

"Well, it's new,' she said defensively.

Earl grinned, pushing black hair back from his pale, thin face. "And you, of course, are tattered and expendable, being all of fourteen years old."

She kicked a bare foot at him, but he dodged back and then joined the others squatting by the fire. "But as well as thanks," he said, "perhaps we owe this gentleman some introductions. This damsel, formerly in distress, is Heather McKenna. He is Wellington Jones, and I am . . . Earl Bedwas."

Heather raised an eyebrow at that, but said nothing. Instead, she studied the newcomer. He seemed to be about the same age as Earl looked, seventeen or eighteen perhaps. His embroidered leather jacket and boots, now drying on the sand, had a slightly foreign look about them.

"I'm Kyle, Kyle O'Mara. I'm a harper, just come this morning from Ireland."

"Ireland," Heather and Welly said together, exchanging excited smiles. Foreign countries always sounded so glamorous, particularly since there were so few still inhabited. At least in Europe and North America.

"Yes, I came to find and join your King Arthur." He looked down, a blush spreading over his already dark face. "You'll be thinking I'm a romantic fool. But over in Ireland we've heard rumors about Arthur's return, about his setting out to unite all of Britain as it was before the Devastation. And . . . and, well, I thought maybe he could use a harper. Kings always did in the old tales."

The three young people smiled and nodded. "I'm sure he could," Welly said. "But if you're headed to Keswick, what were you doing on this beach?"

"Oh, well, I asked a man at the harbor how best to get to Arthur's town, and he said there was a small party from Keswick heading back there soon, and they'd gone off toward this beach. I was looking for them but didn't see anyone except you kids. You didn't notice them, did you?"

After an awkward silence, Earl said, "Actually, it was probably us the man was talking about. We came from Keswick on business and were going to start back this afternoon, except we got a little diverted trying out the new ball."

Kyle's expression wavered between pleasure and skepticism. "Isn't it a little dangerous for, eh . . . young people to travel unescorted all that distance?"

"Oh no," Welly answered. "Not really. Now that Arthur's united Cumbria, his patrols keep down the brigands and slavers. And the muties don't cause much trouble."

"Oh, that's good to hear. And your, eh, business is all taken care of?"

"Oh, I think so, isn't it, Earl?" Heather said, as the older boy nodded in response. "Yes we had some people to talk with, and we wanted to inspect the new port. There hasn't been a really good one here since before the Devastation, when the coasts were higher. But the Duke of Ravenglass made an alliance with Arthur last year and agreed to build up the port. What did you think of it?"

"I was impressed, and there seems to be lots of other building going on."

Earl nodded. "These Cumbrian dukedoms used to fight a lot among themselves. But now that Arthur's united them, there's time for building and for trade." He stood up, brushing sand off his trousers. "Maybe we'd better get going. Are you dry enough?"

Kyle felt his clothes. They were stiff with salt, but dry. "Yes, I am. That was a fine fire you built, and with very little fuel, too."

"Eh . . . yes, thanks. I have a . . . . knack for that sort of thing. Have you a horse?"

"No. I tried to find one but was told the king was assembling them all in Keswick, at least the tall ones. Why is that?"

Welly spoke up, feeling on safe ground with questions of military strategy. "He's building a cavalry. And he's choosing all the taller horses to breed with each other so we can start getting real warhorses again, like in the old days."

Heather reached for her boots, brushing off the dried sand. "We left our horses up by the dunes. Welly's and mine are probably too small, but there ought to be a little extra room on Earl's. His legs are so long he needs an extra big horse." She grinned broadly.

Kyle stood up. "Well now, I would certainly appreciate your company, if I'd not be too much bother. It really is fortunate I fell in with you."

Welly chortled. "I thought it was Heather who did the falling in."

Kyle retrieved his bag and harp from where he'd dropped them on the beach, and together the four trudged through the sand up to where the horses were grazing on clumps of coarse coastal grass.

Soon, with the young Irishman riding on the rump of Earl's black mare, they set off inland. At first the valley of the River Esk was wide enough for several farms. Beyond low stone walls, the hardy short-season grain had just been harvested. It was late August, and the first snows had already blown down from the ice-encased north.

Then the fells crowded closer together, and the narrow road rose more steeply. The land, bare of all but coarse gray-green grass, was inhabited here only by dark-wooled sheep. Occasionally shepherds appeared, armed with fur wraps against the cold and spears against fell dogs and muties. A chill wind buffeted the fells, and the early dusting of snow, swirled it into the air and snaked in wisps across the road. The bleak stillness was broken only by the sound of their own passage, the bleating of sheep, or the lonely call of some rare fell-land bird.

The road itself was old, having been the main route into the British lakelands since long before even the Romans came to the islands. But now the once-paved surface was pitted and crumbling. Often, despite their careful three-toed agility, the small, shaggy horses were forced to thread it single file.

Throughout the day, the sky remained gray, not as much from cloud as from the high haze of bomb-stirred dust that after five hundred years was only now beginning to thin. Behind it, a veiled sun was sinking into the now distant smear of the Irish Sea, when Earl finally called a halt for the night.

They had already crossed the first pass and dropped into the desolate vale beyond. Where a dark, icy stream gurgled under a bridge, Earl led them off the road to camp within the low stone walls of a sheep fold.

Kyle was content to let the boy take the lead in this. And he'd enjoyed listening to Earl point out features along the way, though his guide persistently sidled away from some of the subjects he'd asked about.

After they dismounted, Kyle set out to collect dried sheep dung for a fire but returned to find that Earl already had an impressive blaze going. They pulled a supper of bread and radishes from their saddlebags, and the young Irishman, burning with questions, could wait no longer.

"Please now, tell me about Arthur and his court and all. Living in Keswick, you must know something about him. We've heard so many stories, even in Ireland. But I confess it's hard to believe that all of them are quite true."

Welly and Heather took on similar expressions, polite but cautiously blank. They deferred to Earl.

Rubbing a thin hand over his beardless chin, Earl asked, "What have you heard?"

"Oh, about how this is the *real* Arthur Pendragon, the one out of legends. About how the old wizard Merlin and a couple of warriors battled monsters and Morgan the Enchantress to make their way to Avalon. And how they awakened the king there and brought him back, magically made young again, so he could unite and bring peace to all the fighting shires."

"Well, that's all true . . . enough."

"But what about the magic? I mean, sure I believe in it; there's a lot of little magic these days. Some people can use it to find lost tools or remove splinters or cure sick sheep. But the stuff these stories talk about is high magic, like graybearded wizards casting spells and people coming and going into Faerie and talking with Eldritch folk."

The Irishman shook his head. "I mean, maybe it's all true. But doesn't it make you uncomfortable? How can normal people get used to having powerful magic workers just walking among them? I don't know that I could."

Tension tightened around the group like a fist. "You could try," Welly said tautly.

Into the dragging silence, Earl suddenly hissed, "Quiet, something's coming."

Kyle was amazed at how suddenly and silently the fire was quenched. But his attention was quickly pulled elsewhere.

From a small side valley came the sound of horses, many horses. The muffled clicking of three-toed feet, the jingle of harness, the occasional clank of metal on leather. A party of armed men. But whose?

two

The Wages of Power

Keeping very still, the four huddled together within the stone enclosure. After the sound and the dark shapes had passed down the valley, Welly whispered, "Were they ours?"

Earl answered. "I doubt it. None were wearing the Pendragon badge."

"But it's too dark to be sure of that," Kyle pointed out.

"I have good night vision," Earl answered simply. "But whether they are brigands or others, an armed party of that size should not be wandering around in Cumbria. We'd better follow and see what they're up to."

"But surely that's not our job," Kyle complained.

"Hey," Welly said, "one of the reasons the Cumbrian dukedoms accept Arthur as king is that he maintains order. And anyone who's sworn allegiance to him has to help in that."

"Besides," Heather added, while quickly saddling her

horse, "wasn't adventure one of the things you came here to find?"

"Well, yes," the Irishman admitted. He refrained from adding that authorized adventure was one thing, but playing around at night with kids pretending to be heroes was another. At the same time, he had no desire to be left in this strange, bleak land by himself.

Soon they were packed up again and on the road, moving eastward. Their quarry was some distance ahead, but although the pursuers gradually gained ground, they were afraid to draw too close and risk being noticed. In the eastern sky, a blurred half-moon cast faint mists of light over the fells.

After threading down the narrow valley, the road rose steeply until there came a brief moment when the armed men were darkly outlined against the gray-black sky. They disappeared over the pass, and the four young people hurried after them.

When they, too, reached the pass, they saw on the slope below a scatter of campfires twinkling through the dark. Silently Earl motioned a halt.

"There's a second troop camped down there."

"Are they more of the same?" Heather asked.

Earl stared into the night. "No. Some of the ones around the campfires are wearing black and gold badges. It must be one of Arthur's patrols."

"Then what are . . . ?"

Welly's unfinished question was answered by a sudden eruption of sound. Out of the dark, from where they had stealthily circled the camp, the first group of armed men broke into savage yells and swept down in attack.

Instantly all was chaos. Around the fires, startled men jumped up, grabbed weapons, and began flailing at the mounted attackers. Noise of battle jarred the cold, silent valley.

"We've got to do something!" Heather screamed.

"What can we. . . ." Kyle began.

Earl turned in the saddle. "Get off," he ordered brusquely. Startled, Kyle slid off the mare, and quickly Earl unfastened the walking stick that had been strapped to the saddle. Raising it over his head, he spurred his horse downhill toward the fight.

Suddenly it seemed he was holding a torch. From the end of his staff, purple flames soared upward, spewing a cloud of glowing smoke. The smoke pulsed with light and life as it rose higher and higher into the air. Then it spread out, beginning to take form and solidity.

In moments, a huge purple dragon was hovering over the battle. Its beating wings stirred mighty gusts of wind, and its gaping mouth reeked of sulphur and glowed with the fires of hell.

Below, men and horses screamed in horror. In moments the mounted attackers were scattering over the hillside. Most of those in the camp hurled themselves to the ground or ran screaming into the night.

After silence began settling onto the hillside, one deep voice rang out from beside a fire. "Look! It's Merlin! Merlin the Wizard. Men of Arthur, that winged beast's only a thing of sorcery—and ours at that!"

The wizard, staff now lowered, rode his black mare up to the large dark-bearded man who'd called back the still reluctant troops. The big man smiled broadly, but even he stayed a cautious distance from the boy. Overhead the dragon was already fading to smoke and blowing away on the wind.

"Well met, Merlin lad." The man turned a nervous, scowling face toward his troops, observing their extreme slowness in returning to the camp. Apologetically he glanced back at the wizard. "They're brave boys, really. It just seems that some of them prefer flesh and blood enemies to magic, even if it does save their skins. I guess they remember your earlier demonstrations. But me, now, I've never been one to say that magic doesn't have its place in an army."

"Thank you, Otto. But I suggest that from now on a few more sentries should have a place as well."

The other frowned but held back any reply, and the boy

on the black horse continued. "Have you any idea whose men those were?"

"None. But a few got themselves left behind with swords in their ribs, so we should find out something."

Welly, Heather, and Kyle had joined the others around a campfire when a soldier reported to Otto that examining the bodies had revealed nothing. "Well, then, bring me that horse you caught," ordered the commander. "Maybe there's some clue in the saddlebags."

A shaggy bay horse was lead up, its eyes and nostrils still wide with fear. Heather got off her own horse and walked over to the animal.

"Poor thing, he's even less used to Earl's . . . unusual tactics than ours are." Gently she patted its nose then moved a hand up to rub behind its ears and down the long coarse hair of its neck.

Otto finished rummaging through the saddlebags. "Nothing! There's not a clue where they're from."

"Oh, the horse is from Lancaster," Heather said without thinking.

"How would you know?" Otto asked sharply.

"Oh, I . . ." she stammered, "I just do. I mean, well, horses from different places have a different . . . look about them. This one's just like those Lancaster horses captured after that border raid last year."

"Hmmm, maybe," Otto said skeptically.

Merlin looked curiously at Heather but intervened. "If Heather says this horse is from Lancaster, Otto, it probably is. She has a . . . good feel for animals. However, if a party of Lancaster warriors has penetrated this far into Cumbria, Arthur must be told immediately. I don't know what your original patrol assignment was, but I suggest you detail a contingent to continue it, while you and the others set out for Keswick by first light."

Otto frowned. "Yes, I suppose that would be best. Come on, let's see how many we lost. Eh . . . will you help with the wounded?"

"If I can. Healing magic is not what I'm best at."

Heather turned to see Kyle staring after the soldier and the wizard. He blinked at her. "You mean Earl . . . he's, he's. . . ."

She sighed. "Didn't the stories you heard mention that when Merlin came back into the world, he was a lot younger, too?"

"Well, maybe something of the sort. But he's just a kid!"

"Yes, in a lot of ways, he really is." She could see Kyle was not comforted. As he turned away, she thought she saw him make the hand sign against evil omens.

Shaking her head, she turned to Welly. He shrugged. "Well, it was worth a try. Guess I'll go see if I can be of some help."

Heather looked again at the captured horse. It had a shallow cut on its withers but seemed to be suffering mostly from fear. She tried to soothe it, but her mind kept drifting back to her friend.

She'd known what Earl had hoped to do from the moment he'd introduced himself with that name, the name he'd had in school before he regained the memory of who he was. He must have hoped that this newcomer would come to know and like him as a person before learning that he was also the wizard Merlin.

It might have worked if he hadn't been forced to thwart this attack publicly. But even then, Heather wasn't sure. For though magic was returning to the world, people still found it very unsettling. And the daily presence of magic workers among them seemed the most unsettling thing of all. The greater the power, the greater the fear and isolation it seemed to bring.

She frowned, abruptly forcing her thoughts aside. Strange powers and social isolation were nothing she wanted to dwell on just now. She hurried after Otto and the others, hoping there was some diverting task for her as well.

The next morning, they were all on the road before the dust-shielded sun had cleared the eastern hills. Kyle now rode the captured horse, willingly leaving Merlin alone on his black mare. The route led sunward past a small frozen tarn, then veered north at Ambleside.

Heather felt uneasy but tried to keep her mind firmly on the surroundings. She smiled at the occasional farmer or herder who waved as the troop rode past. She studied Thirlmere as they clopped along its eastern shore. With its long narrow surface already mottled with ice, it looked like a huge molting snake stretched beneath the fells.

But her thoughts kept sliding back. Finally she faced them. How *had* she known that the horse was from Lancaster? She had touched the horse and felt its fear and longing to go home. And she'd almost seen the route it longed to take, the winding tracks that led back—to Lancaster.

She shook her head to banish the picture. This wasn't the first time this sort of thing had happened. In a way, it was exciting, like suddenly discovering you had some little skill that others didn't—like running faster, maybe, or being good at sketching. But this wasn't some ordinary little skill, and when she stopped pretending that it was, it frightened her.

It also made her feel very alone. Maybe this was the time. Maybe she should ride up beside Welly and talk to him about it. But though he was her oldest friend, she knew he wouldn't understand this. And Earl, a friend just as close, might understand too well. Frightened again, her thoughts shied away. Desperately she admired the landscape.

Toward evening they cleared the final pass and dropped down to Derwentwater and the little town of Keswick. Against the dark backdrop of the fells, smoke from cooking fires was already rising from the clustered buildings at the lake's north shore. Before reaching the center of town, they turned off at the old manor, for five hundred years home of the dukes of Keswick and now headquarters of Arthur, king of Cumbria.

It had not been far from there that, two years earlier, Arthur along with herself, Welly, and Earl, had emerged from Avalon. At first, the local people had been skeptical of the young blond man and his claim to be *the* King Arthur.

But a dramatic and, to many, still frightening demonstration of Merlin's magic had convinced them on that score. And as the Duke of Keswick had recently died without an heir, the people of the town were willing enough to take on this vigorous, personable young leader. Arthur, through diplomacy and a few strategic battles, had since brought all of Cumbria behind him and this summer had extended his realm beyond the eastern mountains to Carlisle.

As their party clattered into the cobbled courtyard, the sound brought people rushing from the buildings. Soon the air was filled with white breath, eager voices, jingling harness, and the stomping of hooves.

A tall blond man strode out of the main hall, his skin as pale and bright as snow in sunlight. Amused, Heather watched Kyle as, with growing understanding, he looked first at the king then back at Merlin. Both were strikingly pale, paler than anyone could be whose ancestors had survived the radiation rained on the world after the Devastation. But no paler than someone should be who had first walked this world two thousand years earlier.

Arthur slapped Merlin familiarly on the shoulder and listened while he and Otto described the battle on the Ravenglass road. Remembering the horse, Heather said nothing. She started to slip away, but decided that might only call more attention to herself. Trying to look small and unimportant, she joined the group around the king.

Arthur was nodding, stroking his short, golden beard. "So, the question is, why were Lancaster raiders that far into Cumbria?"

"Spies probably," said Reginald, Duke of Ambleside.

"Yes," the king agreed, "but would they risk that much provocation on their own? Up to now, Lancaster's seemed anxious to stay out of our way."

"And you are suggesting . . . ?" Otto asked.

"That they might have formed an alliance with someone and agreed to do the scouting."

"An alliance with Morgan, maybe?" Welly suggested from the sidelines. Arthur frowned, then raised a questioning eyebrow at Merlin, who was standing somewhat away from the others.

The wizard shook his head. "No, there's no feel of Morgan about this. These were ordinary men on an ordinary mission."

Relieved, Arthur nodded. "And we've heard nothing of Morgan or her minions meddling this far north—not yet, at least. No, I was thinking more of Queen Margaret."

"The Queen of Scots?" Duke Reginald said. "That would be awfully bold of her."

"I suspect the new Scottish queen is a very bold person indeed. Look at all she's done since succeeding her father."

"True enough," the Duke agreed. "But if we're going to debate strategy, let's do it inside. It's starting to snow again." Fussily he brushed snowflakes from his full, gingery beard.

The others laughed and headed up the broad steps to the arched entrance of the hall. Welly led Kyle up, but Heather hung back. Then she saw Merlin walking toward her, a questioning look on his face. The fear clutched at her again, and she hurried after the others.

"Come on, Earl," she called tautly over her shoulder. "Let's go hear if the new harper can sing. Haven't you been saying that Arthur needed a bard?"

Merlin's look of concern dissolved into a wry smile. "Yes, but I suspect this one is learning that magic and legends are a lot more comfortable in song than in reality."

Heather shivered and nodded in silent agreement. Behind them, the August snow began falling in earnest as the two walked into the kings's hall.

three

Stirrings

Whatever his own misgivings, the young harper impressed his hearers with both his voice and his skill at the harp. The background necessary to be bard for this particular king, however, was clearly lacking, and Arthur assigned Welly and Heather to fill the Irishman in on events of the last two years.

For the most part, these sessions were enjoyed by all three, but whenever the harper's questions turned to magic, Heather quickly changed the subject. And although he now knew the story of Merlin's ancient enchantment and his return to childhood in a magical attempt to preserve his life, Kyle did not seem to find Merlin's appearance as a gangly teenager to be the least reassuring. Like many others, he gave the wizard a wide berth and spoke to him as little as possible.

One evening at supper, however, Kyle found himself seated beside Merlin. Cold and dark hung among the rafters of the dining hall, but underneath, the air was rich with the fragrance of potato soup and freshly baked barley bread. In noisy conversation, a dozen of the king's closest followers crowded onto benches around an old oaken table, a rare piece of furniture that had somehow escaped being burned for heat in the post-Devastation years.

When, as usual, the subject of next season's battles came up, Kyle hesitantly asked whether they couldn't use Merlin's magic to help plan their strategy.

The wizard frowned at the harper, but when Kyle visibly cringed in response, Merlin softened his reply. "Yes, no doubt it would be very convenient if I could just go into a trance and tell you what Queen Margaret or her allies are planning. But I can't. It doesn't work that way."

"But," Kyle protested, "the old stories say you used to prophesy for Arthur."

The king laughed and passed the tureen of soup down the table. "He's got you there, Merlin. Admittedly, you didn't do it often, but you *did* occasionaly come through with some pretty good ones."

Exasperation crawled across Merlin's face. "Yes, but prophecy is not my strong point. Nobody seems to realize that there are many kinds of magic. Prophecy is a specialty, and with those for whom it doesn't come easily, it requires specialized equipment. I don't have that now."

"So you can't even tell what we're having for dinner tomorrow night?" Kyle asked incredulously.

"Not without talking to Cook."

"Then what use is there in being a wizard?"

The large chunk of bread on Kyle's plate suddenly vanished and reappeared on Merlin's. "Oh, it has its uses," he said, taking a leisurely bite. The harper blanched and concentrated on eating his soup.

When the early snow had melted, the second promised consignment of horses arrived from the allied dukedom of Carlisle. The next morning, most of the town came out to the king's horse meadows to examine the new arrivals. This town of farmers and herders took a proprietary interest in everything their king did. And despite earlier scoffing, they now had no doubt about his ideas for building up the horse population. Arthur's dominion had spread, at least in part, because of his new mobile cavalry.

Heather and Welly joined the others by the horses. In the watery sunlight, the grass glinted silver with frost and crunched underfoot. The air smelled of horse and excitement. Appraisingly their eyes scanned the shaggy beasts, picking out those whose size or other throwback features might breed improved warhorses.

"What do you think of that bay stallion there?" Welly asked, as they hung over the stone wall of the corral. "He's almost as tall as Arthur's gray."

"He's a beauty," Heather agreed. "But he doesn't seem very content. Maybe, once he gets to know the place, he'll calm down a bit."

"Yeah, but whatever their temper, you can bet we won't get tall ones until everyone else is mounted on one."

"We *are* still kids."

"We've seen as many battles as most of the rest!"

"But you don't look the part," Merlin said, coming up behind them. "This war business is largely image. Ferocious warriors on big horses scare people more."

"But I can make terribly ferocious faces," Welly said, producing an expression that made him look like a demented toad.

Merlin laughed. "As my mother used to say, watch out, or someday your face will freeze like that."

Welly and Heather exchanged startled glances. Somehow, they'd never thought of their friend as having had a mother. But before they could pursue the matter, a commotion arose near the king, and the three went over to find the cause.

"Certainly I can talk with him now," Arthur was saying to one of his retainers. "Didn't he come all the way from Bassenthwaite to talk with his king?"

Though Bassenthwaite was actually no great distance, the statement made the tousled peasant nearby swell with pride. Self-consciously straightening his clothes, the young man walked up to the king. He attempted a bow, looked up, and was struck speechless as he realized the tall, fair man a few feet from him was actually King Arthur.

The king stepped into the spluttering silence. "You have a message from Bassenthwaite?"

"Yes, Sire, King Arthur, Sir. We lost some sheep, a third of our flock, Sire. We're a poor valley, Your Majesty, and it's a real blow. The shepherds lost them in the last storm, and we haven't been able to find so much as a scrap of wool since. And what with the fell dogs and muties, it worries us, you see, Sire."

"Lost sheep," Arthur said flatly. Then he smiled. "Well, young man. Why don't you go with this gentleman here. He'll see about getting you some refreshment, while I discuss this with my advisers."

"Oh, yes, thank you, Your Kingness." The man bowed and stumbled backwards until he was led away.

"Lost sheep!" Arthur exclaimed. "I have horses to work with before the next snow, the couriers from Carlisle brought alarming news about the Scots, and now I'm to look for lost sheep."

"Remember, Arthur," Merlin cautioned, "the first thing any conqueror must do is keep the homefront happy."

The king turned on him. "Have you any idea, Merlin, how difficult it is to take advice, particularly correct advice, from a beardless boy?"

"If you like, Sire, I could conjure up a beard until my real one grows in."

"No, please don't. It would look ridiculous. All right, let's get some of those townspeople to form a sheep-hunting party. Make it a prestigious royal commission."

"Could I go, too?" Heather asked. She enjoyed horses but had a special feeling for sheep. They were dumb and helpless, yet hardy and stubborn as well.

The king looked at her a moment. "All right. Several parties would be more efficient, and you're good with animals. And yes, Welly, don't ask. You go, too; you're getting to be a good weapons man. But don't you ask, Merlin; I need your advice on this business with the Scots." He looked around. "Kyle, why don't you go with them. Your songs could use a little more local flavor."

Within an hour the sheep hunters set out. The largest group headed north with the shepherd, but Heather said she wanted to look west of broad Bassenthwaite Lake.

"Well, Miss," the shepherd said, "I don't really see how they could have gone that far. But suit yourself. The more eyes the better."

So the party of three headed where the western fells bore down on the valley, their high peaks trailing thin banners of snow in the wind. Heather trudged along silently, trying to think about sheep, trying to think like sheep. Welly thought more about horses and how he wished he were riding one now, a large white one.

Dutifully Kyle looked around him, trying to find words and feelings for the wild mountain landscape, for the sheets of wind-chopped water glinting like dull silver in the misty light, for the brave rock-walled fields, and for the high fells baring the bones of the earth to an empty sky.

Suddenly the sky was no longer empty. Hollow haunting calls fell from it, from the wedge of dark specks cutting across the expanse of gray. "Look," Kyle called. "Those must be geese. I read that they used to fly like that."

"Geese," Heather breathed, listening to their wild music. "Then they aren't extinct. I hope Earl sees them. He gets so depressed sometimes about the things that are gone."

After a time, staring into the sky, Welly cleared his throat. "I hate to mention it, but if it's sheep we're looking for, they'll be on the ground."

"Welly! You have no romance in your soul!" Heather exclaimed.

"I do, too."

"That's true, you want a white charger."

Welly blushed, and taking off his glasses polished them furiously on his jacket front. "They don't come in white anymore," he muttered.

Heather laughed apologetically. "Well, you'd look dashing on one if they did." Tugging thoughtfully on a braid, she continued. "Let's go that way. I feel . . . I mean, I think that's a good place for sheep." She pointed to where several fells folded down to form a narrow valley.

"Wherever you say." Welly jammed his glasses back on.

They climbed into the mountains until Heather finally stopped at the mouth of a small gorge. A frozen ribbon of water trailed from it into a loudly gurgling beck.

"Up here."

"Here?" Kyle said skeptically. "See any footprints?"

"No. Yes. Come on."

The snow here had melted, and between the rocks the grass was dry and springy. As they climbed the steep gorge, Welly contemplated the ancient term "wild-goose chase." Now that he'd actually seen geese, he wondered if "wild-sheep chase" wouldn't be more appropriate.

Heather turned into an even narrower ravine. Welly, puffing up behind her, was about to protest when the cold breeze brought the sound of sheep bleating.

Kyle stopped, bewildered. "How did you know?"

She answered tensely, without turning around. "I just . . . did. Come on, let's try to drive them back to the valley."

After several minutes, they'd had little success. Every time they closed on a dark, woolly animal, it moved off—in the wrong direction.

Suddenly Heather stiffened and spun around, looking at the rocky crags above. "Hurry! We've got to get them away. There are fell dogs about."

"Nonsense," Welly asserted. "If there were, these sheep would be all worked up."

"Well, there are, and *I'm* worked up. Get them moving!"

Their increased frenzy finally turned the sheep in the downward direction. But they were only halfway to the main beck when the sound of growling rolled down at them from behind.

The sheep broke into panicky flight. Heather looked back. Two grizzled fell dogs sprang out from behind a rock. Red tongues lolled between bared yellow fangs.

Welly and Kyle pulled out their swords and ran back to her. But Heather just stared at the animals, her gaze intense and cold. The dogs' eyes were locked on hers. The animals crouched for a spring that never came. Slowly the crouch turned into a cower. Bushy tails slid between their legs as the dogs slunk backwards into the tumbled rocks.

For a moment no one said a word. Then Welly whispered, "They'll be back."

"No," Heather said, suddenly relaxing and turning around. "They won't. But we'd better go after those sheep, or they'll run all the way to Borrowdale."

By the end of the day, the sheep were back with their people. Though Heather herself said nothing, the story of the remarkable rescue spread rapidly.

That night, after dinner in the king's hall, Kyle brought out his harp and sang a new song. It carried in its melody the longing call of wild geese and the sound of wind over barren rock. And the words told of a woman of power and her touch with creatures of the wild, her touch of caring and command.

Heather listened, looking paler and paler. She kept her eyes down but could feel the gaze of others on her. A faint noise of shifting bodies told her that the space between herself and those seated near her was widening. Before the harper finished, she slipped out of the room. A minute later, Merlin followed her.

He found her in the old garden below the hall. She was huddled on a stone bench beside a large carved urn. Tears glistened on her cheeks.

Sitting quietly beside her, he reached out one thin hand and touched hers. "This has been going on for some time, hasn't it?"

She nodded, then words tumbled out. "Yes, for months, a year maybe. Oh Earl, everything's changing so, inside and out, and it frightens me. Tonight . . . tonight he called me a 'woman of power.' But I'm not! I'm not a woman; I don't want to be. And I don't want any power!"

Sagging against his bony shoulder, she sobbed violently.

He looked down at the quivering plaits of her honey-colored hair. His voice was pained. "Heather, in this world you are a woman. You don't *choose* to grow up any more than you chose these gifts. And power is a gift, though it comes unasked and often unwanted. You cannot deny it; all you can do is try to understand it and learn to use it, instead of letting it use you."

"Oh Earl, I don't know. It makes me so . . . different. It cuts me off so."

In the dark, Merlin sighed. "Don't I know that. Magic is the loneliest gift in the world."

"That's what I mean. I don't want that, not now. I mean, when I was at Llandoylan I was awfully lonely. I didn't fit in. I tried pretending that I didn't care, that I didn't need the others. But now, since we've come to Keswick with Arthur, I do have a place. I belong. How long will that last if people start thinking I work magic, even a little?"

Merlin stared down at his own clenched hands. Then he raised his head, a grim smile on his face. "I understand, Heather. Believe me, I understand. But I don't think it need be like that anymore. The world has changed. Magic is cropping up everywhere now. It might have been latent in your family for generations, and nobody knew because it wasn't the season for it. But the seasons have turned."

A smile quivered on her tear-streaked face. "I don't know. Maybe that makes a difference. I can hope, I guess."

Merlin continued, trying to be cheerful. "Come now. Tomorrow, if the weather holds, I'll take you to a place of power where we can get a feel for what you have and for how to deal with it." He looked at her almost pleadingly. "Is that all right?"

"Yes," she whispered after a silence. "I really can't handle this any longer—not alone."

Hesitantly he squeezed her hand.

That night she lay awake a long while, trying not to think about sheep and fell dogs and the frightening powers that bound her to them. She succeeded only when sheer exhaustion pulled her into sleep.

four

Visions of Power

Heather woke to gray light seeping through the parchment-covered window beside her bed. She slipped from beneath her wool blankets, shivering as bare feet touched the cold stone floor. Quickly she padded over to the one window, which retained three of its ancient glass panes. Scraping impatiently at its ferns of frost, she squinted out for a glimpse of what the day was like. Nothing but gray.

Annoyed, she unlatched the casement and flung it open. Cold mist swirled in, and with it came recollections of yesterday and plans for today. She slammed the window shut. But the memories remained.

Reluctantly she dressed. Every movement was weighted with dread, with a feeling that she was about to step through a gate, a gate that opened only one way. Thoughts of what might lie on the other side were frightening enough. But what really chilled her was the thought of never getting back.

When she finally dragged herself downstairs, she found Merlin waiting for her by the dark fireplace. It was too early in the season to burn precious fuel, and the hall seemed cold as a tomb.

Heather walked toward him, wondering suddenly if she looked as frail and drawn as he did. Is that what magic did to a person? Did it drain them, did it eat them up inside? She shuddered with a confused surge of fear and pity—pity for her friend, fear for herself. Somehow she managed a wan smile as Merlin handed her a bowl of warm porridge.

He motioned her to a stone bench and sat down beside her. "Most of the others have already left to work with the horses. I told them we had other plans."

She said nothing, making herself think only of the rough feel of the pottery, of the fragrant steam, and the nutty taste of each mouthful.

But soon they were putting on their hooded, fur-lined jackets and stepping into the cold gray of the courtyard. The mists had risen from the buildings but still shrouded the surrounding fells. Bleakly Heather looked into the grayness.

"It's not far from here," Merlin said as he headed for the gate. "We'll walk. Horses don't like this sort of thing."

They're not alone, Heather thought.

They trudged up the main road out of town. Keswick, always a small town, had not suffered much from the social collapse of the Devastation. The population had dropped sharply, but the survivors had managed to raise the few crops and sheep that had developed resistance to cold and radiation. The mountains were defense against mauraders, so the citizens of Keswick had never needed to wall in their town. With the arrival of Arthur, however, activity had increased, to house and feed his growing army and to rebuild the more important roads.

The road Merlin and Heather took was one of these. But soon they left it for an old sunken farm lane running between two stone walls. The hedges and wildflowers that once would have softened the stark gray stones had long ago vanished.

Their climb brought them into the mists again, and Heather clutched her hood around her. Her thoughts were as dismal as the setting.

"Here we are," Merlin said. Heather jumped, realizing this was the second time he'd said that. Dutifully she looked around, and her heart nearly stopped. Ahead of her on a bleak hilltop, hulking gray shapes seemed to move in and out of the mist. Her throat went dry.

"I thought stone circles were . . . dangerous," she said hoarsely.

"You're remembering the one on the Devonshire moor. Yes, some are, but they are also places of power. Almost any really old site is. Ancient peoples built where they did, to make use of the power. True, it can attract other unsavory things, like the wraith we met in Devon. But I've checked this place out. The only spirits here are sheep."

Heather looked more closely and saw that some of the gray shapes were indeed moving, and one was rubbing its back against a rough, tilted stone. She certainly felt no menace about the place.

Slowly they walked forward. Some of the stones were missing, and some had toppled over or were leaning at crazy angles. Most of the unworked boulders were no taller than the two of them.

Merlin stepped into the circle. Heather took a deep breath and followed. He stood, head tilted, as if listening to some distant sound. Then he turned to Heather.

"The power here is a gentle kind—earth power mostly. I don't really know what sort of magic you have, but we should be able to tell something there."

He walked off to one side, where an inner rectangle of stones stood. "Ah, this should do," he said, squatting down beside one of the fallen stones. With a sigh of resignation, Heather joined him.

Centuries of weathering had hollowed a shallow depression in the stone, and now it was filled with rain water. Merlin patted the ground, and she sat beside him. "Reflective surfaces are one of the simplest magic tools. They help focus the sight."

"Here, put your hands on each side of this pool. Like that, fine. Now, just look into it. Let your mind go free. Just look at the surface, at the reflections, and at the depths beyond them."

Heather felt foolish. She looked between her hands and saw a hole in a rock filled with stagnant water. The only thing reflected was the mist and the gray sky above her.

She looked and looked until her eyes ached. Her mind tired of even thinking about what she was supposed to do, and she just stared. Eventually he would tell her to quit, and they'd go home.

The reflected mists swirled and thickened into heavy clouds, then suddenly parted, revealing a scene below. She cried in alarm, but the cry was the cry of a bird, a graceful gull with pure white wings.

Bright, clear sunlight sparkled on the water below. The estuary of a great river, it was dotted with boats, some small and active, some huge and quiet in their docks, others sliding majestically along the water.

The gull tilted its wings and soared away from the river, over a great city. The city stretched in all directions, its buildings towering into the blue sky. Windows glinted like jewels in the sun. The noise of rumbling activity rose muted and distant as the gull glided on.

Below, trees replaced buildings. Grass swept in a green wave over the crest of hills. Tiny figures moved over paths and open space. Suddenly their faint voices were drowned under a discordant wail, a piercing cry that swelled to fill the world with its alarm.

The gull veered from the noise and rose up and up, upward toward the sun. Abruptly the sun's brightness and heat consumed the sky and the bird and all creation.

Dizzyingly the brightness faded, and the wings that seemed to carry her were black, a dusty, sullen black. The cry was the hoarse cry of a crow as it glided through the cold gray air. Below, the plain was bare except for wisps of snow harried by an icy wind.

Under a shrouded sun, the bird circled. Below now were two great clusters of figures. Armies. There was little movement—a time for scavenging. Lower and lower the crow dropped. Figures sprawled motionless on the ground, upturned faces blank with terror and death. The bird screamed.

And screamed. Heather found arms around her, shaking her as her own screams faded from the air.

"Heather! Come back!" Merlin's command quavered with worry. She sagged in his arms.

"I'm all right, I think," she said faintly as he helped her lean back against a stone. "Oh Earl, is it always like that?"

"It depends on what you see. The more alarming the vision, the more alarming the experience. But tell me what you saw, that is, if you're up to it. I don't want to . . ."

"No, I can tell you. Only the end was really awful, and the middle maybe. But mostly it was beautiful—and confusing. I really don't understand what I saw."

With Merlin huddled beside her in the misty cold, she described her vision. At last she drew toward the end. "The armies were spread out over the plain, but when I . . . when the crow flew lower, the warriors were lying still as death, all over the ground. Earl, I knew some of them! People from here, part of Arthur's army."

She began sobbing again against his shoulder. "Oh Earl, what did I see?"

He frowned, shaking his head. "I don't know. These things can be so confused. Past and present and future, or simply allegory, all muddled together. But . . ."

He was silent until Heather prompted him. "Yes?"

"There's something about it. Somehow it's the same sort of thing I've been sensing. A feeling, a foreboding that's been growing ever since we came out of Avalon with Arthur. It's as though the same cycle is beginning again. An endless, compelling, fatal cycle."

"I don't understand."

"Heather." He sat forward, looking at her tear-smeared

face. "Once before, Arthur worked and fought to build a united, peaceful world. He succeeded for a while, until hatred and warfare tore it apart. Later others built on what he had done, and civilization grew—but so did the wars and hatred until they blasted us back to this." He swept a hand angrily across the shrouded sky.

"The world is different now," he continued. "There are new forces moving it. Still, though, much is the same, too much. I have this dread that the end will also be the same. We will build and create, and in the end it will all be destroyed. Maybe this time with no remnants left."

Heather shuddered, haunted by snatches of her vision. "Earl, with your power, isn't there something you can do?"

Frustrated, he slammed a fist against the stone. "I don't know! In this new world, magic has changed somehow, too. My spells and tricks seem to work, yet it's as though I were using an old, dying language, an archaic dialect. I can make myself understood by yelling loud enough, but there's a new language, a new magic abroad, and I don't understand it.

"Once I could prophesy, as Arthur said. I had a silver bowl that I made myself, working spells and power into the design. In it I could sometimes glimpse possible futures and help direct the present to the right course. If I had that bowl now, perhaps I could do that again. But it's long lost, and I don't even know if it would work in this new world. Yet I don't know what else to try! My ideas are as old and dead as the world they came from."

He huddled into his cloak, resting his head dejectedly on his knees. Now Heather found herself comforting him.

"Come on, Earl, you'll work it out. You're young now, just like this world. I haven't any idea how to deal with whatever magic I have, I'm not sure I even want to. But I know you can use your power. You'll find something."

He looked up, smiling gratefully, then shaking his head. "Here I am, Merlin the Wizard, just as insecure as any other teenager." He squeezed her shoulder, then stood up. "Well, we did find out one thing."

"We did?"

"The nature of your magic. You didn't see those visions, whatever they were, by yourself. You saw them through the eyes of animals. The events with the horse and the sheep, those were tied to animals, too. What about the other times you mentioned?"

"Oh, well, . . . yes, maybe so. I found where the rats were nesting, and I knew that the gatekeeper's horse was dying, and I really found the necklace only because of a spider."

Merlin was stamping his cold feet, trying to bring some life into them. "That's it then. Unfortunately, I'm not very adept at animal magic. I'll help where I can, but you'll have to pick up a lot on your own, I'm afraid."

Heather stood up, turning her head to hide her scowl at that suggestion. Sighing, she brushed the dead grass from her trousers and followed him out of the stone circle.

Mists now hid only the peaks of the surrounding fells. A cold, damp wind carried the contented sound of sheep, talking to each other and tearing out mouthfuls of coarse grass.

As they passed the last tilted stone, Merlin looked at his companion, then glanced away shyly. "I am sorry, Heather. I know this still must be very upsetting. Power always is. I wish I could make it easier for you. But I have to confess, I am glad to have someone to share it with."

Heather tried to smile in reply, but she was too confused to bring any words with it. She wasn't convinced she wanted loneliness, whether shared or not.

five

Winter's Tales

Before winter fully cut off Cumbria, closing its passes, word came to Arthur from two distant trouble spots. Messengers from the Duke of Carlisle reported that Queen Margaret had led her troops south from the frigid borders of the Scottish ice fields. After rampaging through Northumbria, they now threatened Newcastle. And Carlisle, which also bordered Scotland, was nervous.

The other news traveled with a group of traders from the Midlands. Arthur invited them into the great hall the afternoon they arrived. Throwing skins on the floor, the merchants spread their merchandise temptingly upon them. There were bolts of finely woven linen, dyed red and yellow, and costly carvings of wood from the southwest, where enough trees still grew for such. But the most treasured items were from the olden times.

Heather was particularly intrigued by ancient glass bottles of amber or green, while others looked over pieces of china and a few scraps of rare plastic. Merlin was drawn to a stack of pre-Devastation books.

The metal worker though drew the most attention. On the cold hearth, he set up his forge and blew a bowl of carefully conserved coals into life. "I search for scraps of metal everywhere," he told those around him. "Ruined cities are best. But you've got to be careful about what you take—nothing too rusty, mind. And you mustn't mix most metals. They melt at different temperatures, see. Sometimes I just heat and rework scraps into spear and arrowheads." He clattered a handful onto the stones, and Arthur and others looked them over appraisingly.

"Or I make new beautiful things, like this fine copper necklace. Look at the delicate patterns, at the red glow of the old sun itself. Now, Your Majesty, surely a treasure like this deserves to adorn a royal throat. You're a single man, I understand, but I can't believe you haven't some young mountain beauty you're thinking of making your queen."

Arthur stood up abruptly. "I am not giving any thought to queens! Being a king is quite trying enough without them."

The metalsmith knew he'd made a blunder. He was a clever man but not a learned one, and was unaware that this particular king had, millennia earlier, bad experiences with one queen. So as not to lose his royal audience completely, the man quickly changed the subject.

"We also, of course, carry news along with our merchandise, and to men of affairs like yourselves, it is often more valued."

"So, what can you tell us of happenings in the Midlands," the king asked gruffly.

"Well, Cheshire and Manchester still glower at each other, and there's talk of a full-scale war between them. Manchester wants more land; it's never had much besides old ruins. But Duke Geoffrey of Chester says it can just look elsewhere.

"Now, let's see . . . oh yes, there's the Duke of Staffordshire who married the King of Nottinghamshire's daughter a while ago. All their children were born muties, and he's just sent his wife back. There's trouble brewing between those shires, that's for certain.

"And as for Wales, the old duke of Glamorganshire died just a couple months past, and now his son's upped the rank and taken on the title of king."

Three in the crowded room suddenly looked at each other and laughed. "King Nigel!" Welly exclaimed. "A royal pain."

The merchant nodded. "Yes, Nigel is the gentleman's name, though as to his personality, I cannot say."

"We can." Heather giggled, thinking of the last time she and Welly had seen the heir of Glamorganshire—tied up on the floor of her bedroom while they made their escape from Llandoylan School.

Merlin cleared his throat. "We three had the opportunity to make the gentleman's acquaintance in school. I think, Arthur, if you're considering forming alliances in Wales, you'd better look elsewhere than Glamorgan at present."

The glass merchant spoke at this. "Well, if it's alliances you're wanting, there are some shires that'll be seeking ties with anyone, what with the goings-on in the East and South."

"You mean Morgan?" Arthur asked sharply.

"Yes that's the witch who's been leading them. Kent's been hers for a couple of years now, but her army's grown. Mostly muties from the continent, they say, them and other things best not talked about. Last year they gobbled up Essex, and this year Suffolk. The shires nearby are plenty worried, I can tell you. Her army's worse than most; they pillage and murder something awful."

An old cloth merchant pushed his way into the knot of listeners.

"Aye, there's strange doings all over the South. There's a boy with us now, come all the way from Devonshire, what has some pretty rum tales to tell. You ought to talk with him."

"Yes, perhaps we ought," Arthur said thoughtfully. "From what I'm hearing, I fear we may have to deal with Morgan before we'd planned. Have him brought in."

A guard slipped out the door and returned with a boy who looked no more than eight or nine. One arm was shriveled, and he walked with a pronounced limp. But his eyes were held high as he approached the king.

"Well, young man," Arthur began, "I'd like you to have a seat and tell us . . . "

"John Wesley Penrose!" Heather suddenly jumped up and ran to the boy, followed closely by Welly. Merlin looked up from a newmade silver bowl he was examining and hurried to join them.

The boy's somber face lit with a smile. "I thought maybe you two would be here. And you, Mister Earl, I knew you would be."

"You did?" Merlin asked. "How?"

"Well, when you stayed at our farm, you told me such exciting stories of King Arthur that, when I heard he had returned, I was sure you'd try to join him, too."

The king grinned at Merlin. "And you, John Wesley, you came all the way from Devon to join us?"

"Yes, Sire. I hadn't anyplace else to go, and from what Earl said of you, I was sure you'd take me in."

Arthur looked amused, but Merlin frowned. "What do you mean, John Wesley? Where are your parents?"

The boy's face clouded, and he looked down at his hands. "They were killed. Remember that bird-cat that attacked our farm? A while after you all left, three more came. They killed everything—my mother and father and most of the sheep and cattle. I hid in the barn under the manure. But they tore up nearly everything."

Heather knelt beside the boy and grabbed his hands, too upset to say anything. Welly could do no better.

Merlin's face rippled with anger. "Those were Morgan's creatures," he told Arthur. "She couldn't abide the Penroses being kind to us."

"It's not your fault," the boy said, his voice thick with suppressed tears. "When I was trying to find my way here, I saw other things like that and worse. Not regular muties, but really awful things. They make the air feel dirty."

The king frowned. "You were right, Merlin, she is calling things from the other world. Hasn't changed much, has she? If there's anything filthy Morgan can deal with, she will."

"And her forces are getting stronger, it seems," the wizard said flatly.

"Yes, as ours must before we confront her."

"Sire," an adviser said, "do we really have to confront this Morgan person? I mean, all her conquests so far are to the south. Surely we aren't threatened by her."

"We are *all* threatened by her. At some time, Morgan and I must meet. Our ambitions for Britain are too much at odds. Ask Merlin. He knows."

But the young wizard was paying no attention. He was once again staring at the silver bowl in his hand and fighting off a sudden wave of dizziness. The bowl seemed to grow and became entwined with interweaving snakes. A vision stirred darkly in its depths, swirling and forming just out of sight.

He gasped and dropped the bowl. It lay on the floor, small and unadorned. Arthur grabbed for him as Merlin swayed over it. "Are you all right? What was it, a vision?"

"No, a vision of a vision. And yes, I'm fine. It's over." He put shaking hands on John Wesley's shoulders and managed a smile. "Well, young man, it looks as if we're going to live some of those stories for real now." He looked around. "Heather, why don't you and Welly see that our new recruit gets something to eat."

Late into the night by the smoky light of torches sputtering in wall sconces, Arthur and his advisers talked of future strategies and alliances. But Merlin's thoughts kept straying to the past, to a good Devonshire couple murdered for their kindness, and farther back, to a silver Bowl of Seeing lost two thousand years earlier.

As winter closed around the lakelands, people and animals huddled together in houses and pens. In hearths, fires were sparingly lit, scarce logs supplemented by dried sheep dung.

Last year, Heather had found this season boring and confining, but at least she had felt part of a whole. Now she wondered if there weren't some slight difference. Was she imagining it, or were some people avoiding her? Certainly, some were paying her more attention than she wanted. She wished she had a place tending the sheep and horses, as John Wesley now did. But instead, she found herself with three eager tutors and too much to learn.

Merlin taught her magic, not the spells he knew, for he said their powers were too different. Rather he tried to teach her how to open her mind to her own power and be sensitive to its messages.

Heather was not an eager pupil. She loved her tie with animals, but the power itself frightened her. Sometimes when she felt it welling up inside her, she would shrink away as if from a venomous snake.

Even Merlin seemed discouraged. "I don't know," he told her once as they sat bundled up in the snowy garden. "You have power, I can feel it. But maybe I'm just not the one to bring it out." He sighed. "And it's not only that our powers are different. I'm simply not attuned to this world's new magic. It has a different source, a source I can't quite see yet. My old powers work technically, but more and more they feel dry and out of place."

He frowned until his dark brows met. "Not that any of this brooding is helping you. At least *your* power, whatever shape it is, is right for your world. But I wish I could at least get some gauge of it. You might be an ordinary village witch, or you might be something more. I just can't tell."

"Then don't try," Heather muttered, then quickly looked up, glad he hadn't heard. She didn't want to hurt him, and it seemed to mean so much to him that she had powers, too.

Other times, Kyle tried to teach her music. She was flattered that the handsome young harper took an interest in her, but she could not respond with much interest in his lessons. He said she had a pleasant voice and could carry a tune, but he seemed to believe it should carry every tune he knew. She liked music well enough, but didn't want to live with it every moment of the day.

Kyle, too, was less than content with her progress. "If you'd open yourself to it more," he complained once, "and let it flow through you, you'd be really good." Frustrated, he ran a hand through his blond hair. "It's all that magic you're fooling with. It closes you off, poisons you for honest things. It isn't natural, you know, Heather. You should lead a normal life, with music, a family, pleasant things. A pretty young woman like you shouldn't darken herself with magic."

"I'm not a pretty woman, Kyle O'Mara! And magic isn't dark. It's just difficult, like music. I'm not sure I'm meant for either."

Whatever spare moments Heather had left, Welly slipped into with weapons instruction. Overweight and nearsighted, he had not been good at weapons in school. But in these last two years, he'd become quite skilled with the sword, though his spear aim wasn't what it could be. At least, he thought, his martial name of Wellington no longer seemed quite so ludicrous.

And what he learned, he wanted to share with Heather, his companion in a good many adventures already. Admittedly he had heard people say that Heather McKenna was getting of an age to stop adventuring and think about marriage. She was, after all, fourteen, and with the difficulties women had bearing live healthy children, girls were encouraged to marry and start becoming mothers as soon as possible. But Welly cringed at the thought of Heather's reaction to that idea were it ever mentioned to her.

Welly was surprised to discover that one of the cook's helpers had similar thoughts about him, the marriageable part anyway. Of course, the idea was absurd. He wanted to stay as he was, with a few girls as friends only. Still, it puffed him up a little to know that a pretty thing like the cook's assistant should think of *him* as a good catch.

At long last, even in Cumbria, winter began losing its hold. Heather, as anxious as anyone to ride on the first sortie, was even happier that her three-part tutoring was tapering off.

One morning John Wesley ran to her to say that the herd's first foal had been born. He still treated her as an old friend and was not put off by rumors of her odd powers. Grateful always for that, she followed him eagerly to the enclosure. The air held a thawing mildness. It carried the sound of trickling meltwater mixed with the pawing and snorting of horses restive at the promise of spring.

The new foal was small and dark, but already it was up on its spindly legs, butting its head under its mother's shaggy belly and gulping down milk. Heather watched the scene with lazy contentment. She could reach out and feel the foal's warmth and security, its simple pleasure in the milk and in the presence of its mother. And she felt the dam's love, pride, and happy surprise. Heather refused to look at this awareness as magic.

She spent the day helping John Wesley fork hay or shovel horse droppings into drying pans. Soon she smelled of horse and sweat. Her thin hair, wisping free of its braids was studded with bits of hay. She was thoroughly happy. No dark musty halls, no conflicting voices inside and out. Just a job to do and the freedom to do it.

In mid-afternoon, she was scouring a stone trough. Raising her head to shove back a strand of hair, she caught sight of Merlin walking down from the hall. Almost at the same moment she saw Kyle heading up the road from town.

A wave of guilt at having avoided their tutoring was swiftly followed by anger. What right had those two to make her feel guilty about what she did with herself? If she never hummed another tune or gave another thought to magic, it was her life!

Angrily she threw down her tools and, crouching low, scuttled along a wall, almost colliding with John Wesley as he limped around a corner with an armload of rope.

"If anyone asks about me," she hissed, "I haven't been here for ages. And tell them it's none of their business anyway!"

Sprinting off behind cover of outbuildings, she cut into town, then took the back way up to the manor. Feelings of triumph were muddled with disgust—disgust that even this petty evasion should give her such a sense of freedom.

Dirty, disheveled, and angry, she crept into the lower garden to find Welly hurling spears at a straw target. He turned and smiled at her, his plump open face showing no signs of inner turmoil.

"Heather, why don't you come here and try. . . ."

"No! I'm not going to. I want to do something of my own for a change!"

"Huh?"

"I'm getting fed up with you people! Merlin wants me to become a sorceress and a hermit, Kyle wants me to stay away from magic and be a singer, and you want me to be some sort of Amazon warrior!"

"Hey, I never said anything like that. You can just be what you want, as far as I'm concerned."

"Oh? Then what should I be? With everyone after me, I can't think. What's your advice?"

"I don't know, Heather. Just go your own way."

She stamped her foot. "Welly, I asked for advice, not wishy-washy philosophy. Why are you always so middle-of-the-road?"

"The middle of the road's often the safest place to be."

"Bah! You're no help. All right. I'll go my own way. I'll do exactly that!"

She stalked off toward the hall. Bewildered, Welly looked after her. What had gotten into her lately? He'd heard Cook say, after watching her fly into another such rage, that Heather was just growing up. It looked more like blowing up to him. And it worried him. He didn't want her to do anything stupid.

He picked up another spear and threw, missing again.

Heather did not go down to supper that evening. She said she had a headache. But actually she felt calm with resolve. She was sorry, though, that she'd lost her temper with Welly. It wasn't his fault. It wasn't even Earl's or Kyle's. It was hers.

Everyone *was* making demands on her. But she couldn't even try to answer them, because she didn't know what she was any more, what she wanted or needed. All right, she would find out.

The first step had to be the magic. She couldn't deny it any longer. Whether she wanted it or not, it was hers. Maybe though, she could control it, channel it into ways that wouldn't ruin her life. But she couldn't do that until she knew its strength. And Earl couldn't seem to discover that. All right, if he couldn't, she would have to. And she'd do it tomorrow.

six

Discoveries on a Mountain

The sky was just pearling with gray when Heather, dressed in fleece-lined trousers and jacket, slipped out to the royal stables. The guard gave her a surprised nod but said nothing. She was one of the royal household and was free to come and go as she wished. If the hour was odd, it was no more so than the girl's reputation of late.

Heather ignored him, and the sleepy stableboy as well. She could no longer doubt that a strained distance had sprung up around her as word of her powers had spread. The answer, she'd decided, was to pretend she didn't care. That's what Earl did, though she suspected it was more pretense than he'd care to admit.

Feeling bitterly alone, she swung onto her sturdy little horse. The misty predawn silence was broken as she clattered through the courtyard and out past the gatehouse. Turning right, she rode down into the sleeping town and out to the lake.

The air was cold and needle sharp. Her breath and the breath of her horse rose about them in white plumes. But signs of thaw were already around. The snow on the road had melted and refrozen into a slippery crust. On Derwentwater the imprisoning ice was beginning to break up. Cracks and dark patches spread over the surface, and mists rose from them, veiling the far shore and the lake's shadowy islands. Along the beach, sheets of broken ice had been thrown up by the waves, looking in this uncertain light like jagged teeth tearing at the mists.

As the road climbed above the east shore, Heather looked over the misty expanse of water toward a distant valley, the "Jaws of Borrowdale." Her goal lay there, among the dark, hunched shapes. She hoped some answers lay there as well.

Her power, Earl said, was something she would understand in time. But she didn't have time. Too much was tearing at her *now*. Was hers the power of a garden-variety witch, meant for healing and foretelling storms? Or was it something more? She hardly cared which; she just needed to know, so she could start taking control of her life.

As she rode on, the shape of Castle Crag, dark against the graying sky, loomed more and more forbidding. Yet it was the best place she could think of to go. Earl had said that the ancients built in places of power, and from a shepherd she'd learned that this spot held one of the oldest sites around.

The lake came to an end, and on both sides the fells crowded into a narrow valley. Ahead of her, the crag loomed like a supernatural watchtower guarding the route to Borrowdale and beyond.

She stopped at a crossroads, trying to recall the old map she had studied. The best route should be to the right. She urged her horse across a humpbacked bridge into the tumbled stone ruins of an abandoned village. Turning south, she headed along the River Derwent, still shrouded in its icy, winter silence. It seemed that the only sound in the whole world was what she brought with her, the jingle of bridle and the steady clop of horse hooves on frozen ground.

In the deep sheltered valley, rare trees grew—a grove, almost a forest, like those in ancient tales. Wind moaned coldly in the branches, and the dark towering pines seemed alive with the hostile spirits of those same tales. She was relieved when her trail began rising again, leaving the trees for the open fells.

The path, steep and rocky now, cut along the base of bare cliffs, their surfaces scarred with the white of frozen waterfalls. As she looked up, one ice cascade seemed to shimmer and flow with fire. Over the eastern fells, a huge reddened sun broke free and sent a tide of ruddy light down the opposite cliffs.

Her horse plodded on, bringing her closer and closer to the pass. Perplexed, she reined in. The map had shown the ascent striking off before the pass. Of course, it was an old map, pre-Devastation, but surely the landscape hadn't changed that much.

Standing in her saddle, she looked around. Then she saw it. The distinctive pattern of sheep walls lay behind her in a hidden side valley. Feeling like a successful explorer, she headed the horse back until the narrow valley floor ended in a tumbled wall. Beyond it the crag rose sharply. With a pang, she realized she would have to leave her horse here. Even his throwback three-toed agility couldn't manage this trail.

Dismounting, she tied the reins to a rock and patted his shaggy flank. He was uneasy; she could feel it. He didn't like being away from his fellows. Suddenly she wasn't sure she did either. This idea had seemed fine in Keswick. Now she was less enthusiastic. True, the people and pressures she sought to escape crowded her like this horse's stablemates, but they were protective too. And familiar.

She looked up at the starkly unfamiliar mountainside, then frowned angrily. She was never going to learn about herself if she huddled in a herd! Scrambling over the wall, she began climbing.

On the crag's face, wind had scoured away most of the snow, exposing bare earth and rock. It was the rock that proved difficult. In times past, this place had been used to quarry slate, and the tailings from the quarries now spilled down this whole side of the mountain.

The slate scree ranged from blue-gray slabs to tiny chips, all shifting and clattering under her as she climbed. It was a nightmare climb. For every two feet she advanced, she slipped back one. The rattling, tumbling noise of her passage seemed an outrage in the icy morning stillness.

Finally, panting for breath, she reached a plateau. Below her, cupped in its mountains like the palm of a hand, lay Borrowdale. Stone walls veined the snowy fields and led to a distant cluster of farm buildings. It all seemed safe and familiar and infinitely more rational than this scarred, wind-swept crag.

Pulling her hood tighter around her face, she looked up and groaned. There was still farther to go to the summit. But at least she had reached the level of the quarries. The hillside above would have proper rocks set in soil. Wearily she continued climbing. If there was a place of power any-where here, surely it would be on the highest spot.

Finally she staggered out onto the summit, then looked around in confusion. There were no signs of ancient forti-fications here. To one side was a cairn of piled stones, but that was the type left by climbers in pre-Devastation times when people did this sort of thing for fun.

Discouraged, she sat beside the scant shelter of the rocky mound. The wind sang mournfully over the cold, bare rocks. Behind her, Borrowdale was obscured by the shoulder of the hill, but to the north Derwentwater stretched beneath its fells like a shattered mirror. At its north edge, light from the rising sun was finally sliding over Keswick. Above the huddled gray buildings, smoke from cookfires blended with the fading mist.

In the great airy gulf between her and her home, a single bird soared. She smiled with delight. Birds were so beautiful, with their grace and their achingly precious freedom. How wonderful if the air and hillsides were filled with them. Earl had told her that once summer days had danced with their song.

She longed to reach out and touch that bird, to share its soaring flight, to. . . . No. She hadn't come here for that, but to touch whatever ancient power still ran in this hill.

With a businesslike frown, she looked around the summit again and noticed that there *was* something unnatural about it. The surface had been flattened and was cupped up evenly at the edges. It was a perfect circle, except where quarries had chewed into the hilltop. Standing up, she walked to where the slope dropped steeply from the built-up rim.

So this *had* been an ancient site, though she hardly felt it bubbling with power. But then, she instructed herself firmly, she was not really trying. She walked to the center of the hilltop, thought a moment, then moved further west to what would have been the center before the quarries left a gap, like a wedge cut from a cake.

Bracing her feet apart, she closed her eyes, spread out her hands, and tried to think of nothing. Earl had repeatedly showed her how. But it was so hard. Stupid little thoughts kept sliding in, silly phrases people had said yesterday or pictures of meaningless, ordinary things. Closing her eyes tighter, she tried to drive these fragments away. But the more she fought, the more willfully they sidled in.

She simply had to succeed! Maybe if she tried to stay cool, cool like the snow around her. Cool, pure, untouched. Slowly she relaxed. Coolness and rest spread through her body. She could feel a faint tingling, a faint distant movement like blood throbbing through arteries far, far below her. It was so far, so faint, and other things kept coming in the way.

Ants moved in the darkness, feeling and smelling the earth, grain by grain moving and shaping it, clearing tunnels in age-old patterns of comfort and purpose. They tunneled and crawled past the den of a sleeping mouse, its pulse slowed, its furry chest scarcely rising and falling, its mind drifting in a single summer thought.

Little things, little lives. Heather felt them first with pleasure, then with annoyance. Where was the power, where was the power they hid? Eyes clenched shut, she wrenched her body forward to another, perhaps better, spot and threw open her mind. This deeper power, when would it find her?

Wildly she flung back her arms, tilting her head to the sky. Suddenly she was slipping, arms flailing like bird wings. Her eyes flew open to see the snow-mantled rock at the quarry's edge buckling and sliding beneath her feet. Her mind screamed. Blue slate and white snow spun past her and up to meet her. A rumbling avalanche of snow and rock poured into the quarry. Then mindless silence settled over the hillside.

Wellington Jones never claimed to have a magical bone in his body. But he was certainly good at worrying.

He woke up just as worried as he'd been the night before. Heather was his best friend, and it worried him that she'd blown up at him like that. It worried him even more the way she'd stomped off threatening . . . what? He didn't know, but she was always one for madcap schemes.

When she hadn't come down to dinner, he had been really worried. To anyone who enjoyed food as much as he did, missing a meal meant a monumental crisis. Her not appearing for breakfast was the last straw. She was being ridiculous now.

He stormed upstairs to her little room in the west end of the building. One of the few girls in Arthur's "Court," Heather had a room of her own, whereas Welly slept in one of the men's common rooms. He hammered at the door. No answer.

"Come on, Heather, open up! I'm sorry if you're mad at me, but at least you could tell me why."

Still no answer. Hesitantly he turned the knob and pushed. The door opened onto a small, silent, and very empty room. He looked at the rumpled bed. It had been slept in, but on the wall behind it, the peg that usually held her outdoor jacket was empty.

"Little silly," Welly muttered. "She's off doing something crazy—and without me!"

In moments, he was down the stairs and running toward the stables. Heather's horse was gone. The stableboy reported she had saddled it before dawn but hadn't said where she was going. Useless lump, Welly thought, not even to ask her. But then, he reflected, if Heather had been in the same mood as yesterday, the stableboy had been well advised to lie low.

A thought struck Welly as he was saddling his horse. He hadn't paid much attention to something Heather said the other day. But was it true? Were people really avoiding her because she had some sort of magical powers? The idea boiled into anger. His two best friends, and people treated them like muties!

As he trotted across the courtyard, Otto called out from a doorway, "What you up to, Welly?"

"Important business," the boy answered, throwing him a serious frown. He didn't want to draw any attention to Heather until he learned exactly what craziness she was up to. That could just make things worse.

The guard at the gatehouse remembered Heather heading down into town. Welly did the same. Threading through the narrow twisting streets, he bashfully nodded at occasional smiles and waves. All the people of Keswick knew the plump, bespectacled boy and the skinny, intense girl as being Arthur and Merlin's first two companions. They'd become something of folk heroes, and that made Welly acutely embarrassed. Fame sounded all right in theory but was proving surprisingly silly in fact.

As he neared the edge of town, he stopped uncertainly. But unless Heather had ridden down to the lake to skip rocks on the ice, she'd probably taken the eastshore road. He turned his horse and was soon rewarded with the sight of fresh tracks in the crusted snow. Of course, they could have been made by another rider, but it was worth taking a chance they were hers.

Further down the road, Welly realized that there were several sets of tracks. His confidence faded. But he plodded on until he came to a spot where a single set left the others and crossed the River Derwent on an old stone bridge.

Most farmers with horses had given them over to the king. Just his luck, Welly thought, if he was following one of the holdouts. Thinking again about wild geese, Welly urged his stocky mount across the bridge.

There was cold and emptiness and then a hint of pain. It felt like nothing worth waking up to. Heather's mind tried crawling back into darkness, but there came a slap on her cheek, wet and warm. A very odd sort of thing, considering that she lay dying in a frozen quarry. Curiosity lifted a single eyelid.

She stared straight into the face of a dog. Wonderful, she thought. Instead of bleeding or freezing to death, I'm going to be eaten. She hadn't the strength to make even basic frightening-away sounds.

But if he wasn't to be frightened, the dog wasn't very frightening either. His fur was black with white splotches, and his mouth, which should be striking her with terror, was grinning, a pink tongue lolling stupidly to one side.

Heather opened her other eye. Correction, there were two dogs. Both equally ridiculous looking. One seemed intent on washing out her ear with its tongue.

"Enough!" she gasped as the other's tongue slurped across her face. Obediently they stopped and, whimpering happily, both dogs grinned down at her.

Well, she'd have to get it over with, she thought, and moved one arm. No searing flash of pain. Slowly she tried to sit up, struggling out of a deep drift of snow. Snow, not rocks, she realized. That's why she wasn't shattered over the hillside.

She looked again at the dogs and almost screamed. It was one dog—two heads, two tails, but one dog.

Weird, really weird. But suddenly she wasn't afraid of them, or it. It clearly wasn't a fell dog but some sheepdog pup that had been born a mutie and abandoned by the disgusted herder. Its ribs showed through the matted fur, but the eyes, all four of them, looked at Heather with trustful confidence. The two tails wagged steadily.

Cautiously, Heather reached out a hand and rubbed behind one set of floppy ears. The other head set to washing her arm.

Who was that dog in mythology, the one that guarded Hades? Cerberus. "You're like him, aren't you?" she muttered aloud. "Only I guess you fall a little short. He had three heads. So I won't call you Cerberus, just Rus.

"You like the name Rus?"

Both tails wagged furiously.

"I wonder if I can stand up. If I stay down here, you'll lick me to death."

She flailed about in the snow trying to bring her legs under her. Then came the jolt of pain. Her left ankle. Had she broken it? Twisted it?

She tried again and almost retched with pain.

"Oh, Rus," she said angrily, "just when I thought I was going to live after all. Now I guess I'll die out here."

The dog whimpered, an odd two-part harmony, and began poking her with a forepaw.

"Quit it, Rus. I can't get up, and you're not big enough for me to ride."

He was whining now and looking at her with such pathetic grins she couldn't help laughing. "All right, I'm not giving up that easily, I'll try again."

Cautiously she pulled her good leg under her, and slowly putting her weight on it, she tried to stand. Swaying, losing her balance in the deep snow, she instinctively stuck out her other foot to steady herself. The pain shot up her leg in a sickening wave, knocking her down into blackness.

Whining, the dog poked around the unconscious heap in the snow.

Several times Welly thought he had lost the trail. The road was getting rocky, often without enough snow for tracks.

But he was following a road at least. The rider before him, he guessed, would probably have done the same. The road climbed out of a gloomy pine grove, then rose steeply along the fringes of the fells. A rocky island mountain, Castle Crag, towered on one side. Cliffs glistening with frozen waterfalls rose on the other.

Finally he made the pass and, shifting in his saddle, surveyed the scene beyond. Borrowdale opened out below him on the left. The old road continued ahead along the base of the cliffs. No tracks led anywhere.

Suddenly his horse shied, and he felt something leap against his leg. Alarmed he looked down, and the thing barked and leaped again. A fell dog, an awful mutie, trying to tear him right off his horse!

With a frightened squeak, he struggled to pull his sword from under his heavy jacket. But the enemy was sitting in the snow, smiling with both of its jaws, wagging both of its tails.

Gods, it was ugly, he thought. But at least it wasn't lunging at him anymore.

The creature barked doubly. Jumping up, it ran several feet away, then stopped, and looked back expectantly.

"That's right, you can leave as far as I'm concerned," Welly said, lowering his sword.

Then it ran at him again, barking, spun around, and ran off a few feet. Welly just stared at it. Was this incredible creature rabid, too?

The dog repeated the performance several times to the accompaniment of multiple barking. Welly shook his head. "I actually believe you want me to follow you. But I can't, I'm looking for someone out here and I . . ."

His gaze had gone beyond the dog, down the direction it seemed to be pointing. At the head of a small, nearly hidden valley, he caught a flicker of movement. A horse switching its tail. Heather's horse!

"She went off that way!" Welly spurred his own horse down the road with the dog prancing and barking ahead. Reaching the old wall, he dismounted and tied his horse beside Heather's. The two animals nickered happily at each other and rubbed noses.

The dog was already through the gap in the wall and peering back at Welly with both heads.

"All right, I guess I *am* going your way. But go on, keep your distance. I still don't like the looks of you."

The dog shot on ahead, occasionally stopping to bark impatiently as the stout boy struggled up the slope behind him. On the shifting hillside of shale tailings, Welly alternated his puffs and gasps with colorful curses he'd picked up from Arthur's troops. Despite the cold, the climb soon had him itching with sweat. It was made doubly awkward by his having to clutch his sword in one hand in case that bizarre dog attacked again.

Finally, gasping and shaking with exhaustion, he stood on the open plateau staring out to Borrowdale. Wearily he looked around and groaned. The summit still rose above.

"Heather *would* go up there." He sank down on a pile of stones. "Well, I can't. Not another inch, not just yet."

The dog was beside him again. Welly was too tired to shake it off when it grabbed his jacket cuff in one mouth while barking with the other. He stumbled to his feet and was relieved to see that the crazy dog wasn't leading him upward but along the level, back into an open gash in the mountainside.

The quarry opened out. Above him, raw slate jutted in jagged slabs against the sky. Snow lay in white splinters among rocky chinks and crevasses and piled loosely over the huge stones at the quarry's base. In the center lay something else, dark and heaped.

"Heather!"

Through the deep snow, Welly ran clumsily toward the figure, but the dog got there first, poking and licking with both tongues.

Heather groaned as Welly stumbled up. "Enough! Let me die in peace."

"Heather, what on earth. . . ? Never mind. Let's get you out of here."

"Who? Welly! How did you . . . ?"

"Your funny-looking friend fetched me. Can you stand?"

"No."

"Then I'll try to carry you. If we take that same awful route, you can probably slide most of the way."

Heather was fully awake now. Her ankle was too cold to feel much. "Uh, Welly. . . ."

"Yes?"

"I'm sorry I blew up at you. I'm a really mixed-up jerk."

"True. But at least you're not a dead one. Come on."

seven

Riding Forth

Welly pushed open a narrow window. Oily lamp smoke coiled out while cool tendrils of evening mist slipped in. He turned back and looked at the sleeping, blanket-mounded figure on the bed.

Beside her, Merlin finished his work and gently pulled the blankets back over her left ankle. Having wrapped her with bandages and spells, he now sat down beside his patient.

The flickering lamp cast odd shadows and angles over his face. Heather moved her head restlessly on the pillow. Her hair had wisped free of its braids. Groggily she opened her eyes.

She smiled vaguely. "It feels better already, Earl. But it shouldn't. I don't deserve it. I should be lying up there on that snowy mountain being eaten by fell dogs."

"No, you shouldn't!" Welly objected. The dog lying beside the bed whined and began licking her limp hand with one of its tongues.

The wizard laughed. "These two would never have let you. You have some good friends, Heather."

"I know I do. All of you. But I don't deserve you. I was such a self-centered, headstrong idiot going off like that."

After a silence, Welly said, "I don't suppose you'd tell us why . . . ?"

Heather blushed and tossed her head. "Oh Welly, I'm not even sure why. I was trying to . . . trying to find out about myself, I guess. I wanted to find out what was in me, what sort of power I have. I was tired of everyone but me knowing what I should do with myself. But it was just a big stupid failure."

"A failure?" Merlin questioned.

"Yes, totally. I went up there because I thought it would be a place of power. Maybe it was, but I could scarcely feel it. All I could sense was the little animals in the dirt below me. I'll bet even village witches do better than that. And they wouldn't be so blind as to stagger around the snowy edge of a quarry."

Merlin stood, looking sternly down on his patient. "Heather, you *are* blind, but not in that way. Sensing those small lives, talking with them, that is not small magic. It's not something great magicians learn as babies, then go beyond. Yours is a large power, I believe that now, but it's a different track of magic from mine. I could have stood on that mountain sensing the major lines of power and completely missed what you felt."

"Earl, if you're just saying that to make me feel better. . . ."

"No, you little twit! Look at this ridiculous animal here. Do you think he just happened on you accidentally? And if he did, do you think a half-starved pup would have led a rescuer to this convenient hunk of meat instead of dining on it? No, you had your mind open to that power, and when you fell, you called out for help. He heard and came."

With both tails wagging vigorously, Rus slipped one head under Heather's hand and allowed Merlin to pat the other. A thoughtful smile played over Heather's face. "Well, if I do have to have power, I guess this isn't such a bad kind. That is, if you're right about all this."

He frowned theatrically at her. "You dare question the judgment of the ancient wizard?"

They laughed as he dropped into his chair and continued. "Anyway, I do have a royal command to convey. You are to get well as soon as possible. I tried to work that into my little healing spells. Arthur has decided to head east to join Carlisle against Queen Margaret and her Scots. We'll be leaving in a fortnight, and you and your battlehound here might want to join us, unless of course, you've decided it's time to stay behind and sew like a demure young lady."

Ducking back from her flying fist, he raised an eyebrow. "That's the message I'm to convey to His Majesty?"

"Phrase it however you want. But I'll be riding with you."

Their once quiet town now bustled with activity. Word had spread like smoke that the king was assembling a warhost. Farmers and shepherds took up whatever weapons came to hand and marched proudly through the passes and valleys toward Keswick. They came from fell and farmstead, from Grassmere, Ambleside, and Windermere, and from the coastal villages of Ravenglass and Whitehaven.

While recovering, Heather watched the flurry of preparation. Excited, half-wild horses were trained, metal scraps were hammered onto leather armor, and in the clanging and glowing of the smithies, weapons were forged or repaired. All the while, provisions for the growing army were gathered and stowed away in wagons and packs.

On a cold day, when snow had turned to drizzling rain, Arthur gave word that they would march on the morrow. News had come that Queen Margaret had conquered Newcastle and forced a shaky alliance on Durham. It seemed likely she would move next against Carlisle, and they could wait no longer.

The morning dawned clear and dry, with the sun rising like a bronze shield behind its pall of ancient dust. The hillside camps were astir early, and soon the valley resounded with protesting horses, creaking wagons, and yelling men.

Excited children ran underfoot, some attempting to slip off and join the assembling troops, only to be dragged away by scolding mothers. Youngsters who had passed into their teens proudly joined the warriors' ranks, their eyes glistening with pride and the reflected adulation of their younger comrades.

There were young men too, and old, and some women as well. Some were veterans of skirmishes between shires, and others had never lifted a weapon. But all felt the lure of fame and adventure, the promise of fighting a grand war as in days of old, and of fighting for a king who came from the heart of legend itself.

At last the army was ready to move. From the manor on the hill, the king's troop issued forth and took its place in the lead. Above them fluttered the banner of Pendragon, the winged gold dragon against a field of black. People who had flocked in from miles around lined the road, pointing out personages of note.

At the head of the troops, clutching the king's standard, rode John Wesley Penrose, his pride as bright as the banner he carried. Just behind on his large gray stallion, rode Arthur himself, the faint sun glinting off his armor, his helmet, and his golden hair.

Near him rode the duke of Ambleside, Kyle the harper, Otto Bowman and others of the king's companions. With them, but in a large island of space, rode a pale young man, his hair the same midnight black as his horse. Strapped to his saddle was a twisted wooden staff. Knowingly, locals told newcomers that this was Merlin the Enchanter. If he appeared far too young for the role, his dark look of brooding seemed suitably daunting.

But while their friend was brooding and remote, Welly and Heather were thoroughly enjoying themselves. From the small troop of musicians marching behind, rose the compelling throb of drums, the haunting call of pipes, and the ferocious, challenging blare of ram's horns. The towering fells echoed with the cheers and music, and Welly decided it wasn't all that essential that one ride a tall white charger to feel heroic and glory bound.

Gradually the troops pulled away from Keswick. The road was soon lined with rocks, not cheering people, but the drumbeats still rolled back from the hillsides, and the soldiers laughed and talked among themselves.

In time the drummers tired, and the army, concentrating on marching, was accompanied only by the sound of its own passage: the stomp of hoof and boot, the creaking of harness, the rumbling of wagon, and the casual scrape and clang of weapon against armor.

Heather looked back at the glinting body of warriors winding dragonlike under the bare fells. Excitement was settling into contentment. With little effort she could feel the determined purposeful thoughts of the horses and the more distant annoyance of sheep as they scattered from the army's noise. She was still unsure of how she felt about her power or of the effect her having it made on others, but for now she willingly laid the question aside.

Rus trotted happily beside her, both heads full of curiosity. There was a great deal to smell, see, and chase along the route, and he constantly ran back and forth, dodging horse hooves and marching men.

Only one thing troubled Heather, and that was the brooding cloud that seemed to hang over Merlin. Finally she urged her horse up to join his. He turned in his saddle with a weak smile but said nothing.

"All right, Earl," she said after a long silence. "What's the matter? You have a toothache or something?"

He laughed dryly. "You know, it is rather like that. Something keeps nagging at me about . . . about all this." He swept a hand through the air along the line of march, and Heather noticed several soldiers duck, thinking the wizard was casting a spell.

She frowned, then pointedly ignored them. "You don't think we should move against Margaret now?"

"No, that's not it, not in itself. Strategically this move makes sense, though in the long run it's Morgan, not Margaret who is the greater danger. No, certainly to unite Britain, Arthur must deal with the Scots first. But, somehow, setting out today with the crowds cheering for the glory and honor of war. . . ." He slammed a hand against his thigh. "We've been on this road before, Heather. And look where it ended!" He jabbed a hand upward at the shrouded sun. Again nearby soldiers flinched.

Heather shook her head. "But what other route is there?"

"I don't know! That's what's eating me. I feel there must be another, one that doesn't lead us off a cliff. But I can't see it! If I could glimpse the future as once I could, or maybe if I could get some grasp of this new power. . . ."

He rode on, silent for several minutes. The cold wind ruffled his hair and the fur of the hood thrown back over his shoulders. Sighing, he looked up at the gray fells. "Yes, the new magic might be the key, or one of them. This world is new, starting again. It's no wonder things are different."

He pointed to a tumble of rocks on a bare hillside. "There's one of the differences now. Do you see?"

"No, where? What . . . oh yes, I see something. It's . . . it's a band of muties! Watching us."

"Yes, muties. Some are mutated only in body you know, not in mind or spirit. They are part of this new world. It's theirs, too, whether we're comfortable with that fact or not. Some will work against us, no doubt, but not others, and in the end Arthur must be their king as well.

"And then there are the creatures of the other world, from Faerie. Doors are opening again to all its many parts. They'll be having more and more stake in what's happening here." He laughed dryly. "Before, I saw those doors closing, magic was drawing to the end of its cycle. But now the powers are coming again; they're new and growing. If only I wasn't so tied to the old world, maybe I could help change the outcome this time, both in the long and the short run. Otherwise, what is the point of my being here?" His last words came as such a shout that even his horse shied. But the wizard hardly noticed.

The army camped that night near Penrith, picking up

another eager contingent of volunteers. Next morning they marched north and by the middle of the third day had reached Carlisle. The town's newly constructed walls showed the people's fear of the impinging Scots.

Arthur camped his troops outside the walls, not far from Carlisle's own army. In the center of the sprawling camp, a large tent was erected and the dragon standard stuck into the ground before it. The smoke of cookfires was rising into the dusk when a ram's horn blared from the gate, and a small troop rode forth led by Clarence, Duke of Carlisle.

When the riders reached Arthur's tent, Duke Clarence swung with arthritic care from his horse and bowed to his High King. Then, smiling, he slapped the younger man on the shoulder.

"By the gods, Arthur, this army is even more impressive than the one you marched against *me* last year. I think even my hothead young generals are thankful now for this old man's wisdom in forming an alliance."

"So are we all, Clarence. You make a far better ally than enemy, particularly considering the enemy we face at the moment."

"Speaking of which, I received a message this morning from Queen Margaret, or as she styles herself, 'Queen of Scots and the Lands of the North.' A little presumptuous, I think, since Carlisle is as far north as one can get without crossing Hadrian's Wall."

"She sounds like a very presumptuous lady altogether. But let's discuss this sitting down."

The flaps on the king's tent had been raised like awnings for the war council of Cumbria and Carlisle. Crowding in, the nobles and generals seated themselves on animal skins. On a stool in the center, Arthur sat near a pile of ancient maps, with Dukes Reginald and Clarence beside him.

The tent was crowded, but the space around the king's young wizard was left free until two even younger figures appeared on the edge of the crowd, and Merlin patted the spot beside him. Welly, Heather, and the girl's alarming dog worked their way through to join him.

Shifting on his stool, Duke Clarence pulled a rolled parchment from his jacket. "Before proceeding any further, Your Majesty, I should pass on Margaret's message, arrogant as it may be."

"Certainly, read it to us all."

The old man unrolled the message and squinted at it closely, " 'To Clarence, Temporary Duke of Carlisle.' " The phrase brought gasps and angry muttering from the crowd. " 'From Margaret II, Queen of Scots and the Lands of the North. In pursuance of the pledge taken by myself in ascending the throne of My fathers, I have led my people from their lands of ice and snow to the heart of English plenty. It is My will that the ancient wall that once divided the Scots from England's northern shires now unite us as a backbone. Northumbria is Mine, Newcastle is Mine, Carlisle must be Mine as well.' "

Again outraged muttering in the assembly. "But there's more." Clarence raised a hand, and the group quieted. " 'It has come to Our attention that you have formed an alliance with a young upstart from Cumbria falsely calling himself Arthur Pendragon. If you persist in refusing generous offers to submit to Our dominion, we must move against you and any demented allies that creep from their hills. We urge your surrender now. Obstinacy and fairy tales cannot prevail against the might and majesty of Scotland.' "

The duke let the parchment roll closed and handed it to the king. Arthur smiled thinly. "Well, it seems that centuries of ice have done nothing to cool Scottish arrogance. Now, shall we see what *we* can do?"

From around him came cheers and laughing boasts of what they would do to Margaret and her Scots. Before the noise subsided into earnest planning, Merlin stood up, his face more pale and drawn than ever.

"Sire, a word. I leave war plans to you and your generals. But remember, our goal is not vengeance or simply to have one shire win against another. It must always be to unite those shires, to unite them for the future against the threat in the South. Defeat of that common enemy must be uppermost. Any strategy that furthers that is wise, any that weakens it is foolish."

"Have you any specific advice then, Merlin?"

The youth hung his head. "No. I cannot see the answers, only the dangers." He looked up again, his face sickly pale. "Too much eagerness for bloodletting may be one of them."

Abruptly he turned and left the tent. The silence was broken by muttered questions about who this pushy brat thought he was and by hushed answers from those who knew. As talk turned to the coming battle, Heather left her place and slipped out.

Cold night had fallen, its stars shrouded by the usual high dust. In the distance, the darkened bulk of Carlisle glimmered with scattered lights. On the surrounding plain, the shapes of men and horses were dark smudges, illuminated here and there by the ruddy glow of campfires. Acrid smoke from burning dung twisted through the chill air along with the sounds of men and horses and the muted clatter of equipment.

Heather asked a guard outside the tent if he had seen Merlin. Making a quick sign against ill omen, he pointed to a thin figure standing alone on a nearby knoll. She frowned as she left the guard. These people, she thought angrily, were willing enough to benefit from magic. They might even use a little about their farms. But they still feared it and those who worked it for them.

"Earl?" she said approaching the shadowed figure. As he turned toward her, the glow of a distant campfire lit his haggard face. Suddenly she wasn't sure why she had come. She certainly didn't want to talk about magic. No, it was he that worried her.

"Earl, you looked awful in there. Are you sick?"

He sighed in the darkness. "I might as well be. It's the same thing, Heather, getting worse. Sometimes it tears at me so, I can hardly stand it."

"But surely you don't think we should abandon this battle? Carlisle's an ally. What respect would people have for Arthur if he didn't help his allies when they need it?"

"I know, I know. But look at the whole picture. Here we've gathered the best warriors and some of the best farmers and shepherds from all of Cumbria. We'll join the same sorts from Carlisle and march against more of the same from Scotland, Northumbria, and Newcastle. And what will happen? Oh, there'll be a Glorious Victory for someone. But hundreds of people will be dead. There'll be that many fewer farmers and shepherds to work this land, and that many fewer warriors to hold out against Morgan and her forces in the South."

Heather shivered, remembering her own past meetings with Morgan. "But what can we do? I mean, right now? You said yourself that Arthur must unite all these little quarreling shires. If they don't acknowledge him voluntarily, how can he do it except by war? If you tell those generals of his not to confront Margaret's army, they'll tear you apart."

"Oh, we can confront her all right. But maybe . . ."

A long silence. Impatiently Heather broke it. "Maybe?"

"Heather, I may need your help, and Welly's, too. Can I have it?"

"What kind of help?"

"Nothing you can't do."

"Yes, but *should* we do it? No, don't answer that. If I can, I'll help. But what is it?"

"I'm not sure yet. Just an idea. If I only had my Bowl of Seeing, we could get some inkling of what this battle has in store. But we may have to act nonetheless."

He laughed and gently squeezed her shoulders. "Thanks, though. I'm suddenly feeling better. Maybe you should play around with healing magic, while you're at it."

With dawn came orders to break camp and prepare to march. During the night, word had come that Queen Margaret was on the move, marching west from Newcastle along the course of the ancient Roman Wall.

Heather crawled from her frost-stiffened bedroll. After three days in the saddle, every muscle in her body ached. She was moving so much like an ancient crone, she was almost surprised to see that her hair hadn't turned white.

Gingerly combing and rebraiding it, she soon joined the bustle around Arthur's tent.

Duke Reginald, his short, squat body planted firmly in front of the king was arguing vigorously. "You're a stubborn man, Sire, if you'll excuse my boldness. But it's a mistake to march out to meet her. We know where she's heading. Stay put, I say, and let her troops tire themselves marching to us."

Arthur ran an exasperated hand through his hair. "That makes sense, Reggie, but think of it from Clarence's point of view. He doesn't know how this battle is going to go. We could lose it or reach a stalemate. Every foot the Scots move into his territory is land they might hold."

"True but . . ."

"Rest assured, friend, no forced march. We'll move just fast enough to limber ourselves up."

The other laughed, but beside him, one of his serious-faced young generals shook his head. "Sire, you said we couldn't know how this battle will come out. But we could, couldn't we, if we asked that wizard of yours?"

Merlin, who had been struggling nearby with the bent clasp of a saddle girth, turned toward them, but Arthur waved him back. "It would be nice, wouldn't it," the king said. "I admit I don't understand magic, but Merlin tells me prophecies are out." He smiled, thumping the general on the shoulders. "Besides, half the fun of these things is the suspense."

But the man persisted. "Well then, how about improving the odds? Couldn't he throw thunderbolts at the enemy, or make them fall asleep, or turn us all into forty-foot giants?"

Merlin sighed and, leaving the saddle, walked toward them. With a wry smile, the king deferred to him.

"Arthur knows just how often we've had this conversation, and the answer's always the same. Magic's not much use on a battlefield. If you'd been with us these last three years, you'd know that magic used simply to frighten tends to scare both sides equally. If I used it as a weapon and started hurling spells or flames at an enemy, it'd likely hit our people as well. And as for turning us into giants, one magician, even a troop of them couldn't maintain an illusion like that for long, not with several thousand pseudogiants running around.

"No, Arthur and I have an arrangement. I understand magic, and he leaves that to me. He understands warfare, and I leave that to him. I'll go along, but only to help here and there."

Arthur nodded. "What this smooth-faced kid is saying, gentlemen"—he dodged a good-natured kick from Merlin—"is that we have to win this ourselves—which is as it should be. How are we going to win and hold a kingdom unless people know we have the strength to do it on our own?"

Heather caught Merlin's eye before he headed back toward his heap of stubborn horse trappings. "But I thought you said . . ."

"Hush." He looked furtively around, then pulled her aside. "I meant it. There's no point in throwing magic *indiscriminately* around on the battlefield. But if we are very, very discriminating, we might turn one thing at least in the right direction."

"Earl, stop being an enigmatic wizard! What do you mean?"

He smiled infuriatingly. "You'll see."

eight

Clash Along the Wall

In three days' time, Heather was to learn what he meant.

The land around them now was bleak and wild. From horizon to gray horizon, it stretched in a rolling plain, bare except for rock outcrops and coarse grass ruffled by loud, cold winds. To the north the land swept upward, rising into a long chain of ridges, like waves frozen seconds before breaking. Dark along the crest ran the remains of the Wall.

Millennia earlier, the Romans had built that wall to set off their civilized empire from the barbarian north. But the empire had fallen, and in time so had much of the wall. Yet now, on the sweeping ridges above the army, a crumbling spine of stone still spoke of ancient order.

As Arthur's army made camp that second night, the sky clotted with thick, gray clouds. Before dark had fallen, snow sifted from the sky, sizzling into cookfires and settling wetly on waiting bedrolls. By dawn the whole landscape was dusted with white. Dark stones standing out starkly now, the Wall snaked silently over the ridgetops to their north.

Heather had no eyes for scenery as she tied heavy leggings over her trousers and fastened on the stiff leather breastplate. As she moved, its fish-scale metal plates tinkled like sinister windchimes. Every few seconds she looked up at the dark smudge that spread slowly toward them from the east. The Scottish army. The enemy.

Nervously she buckled her short Eldritch sword about her waist, recalling the first time she had used that weapon after they'd found it in the ancient Eldritch wreck. Then she had faced an uncanny army of Morgan's. This Queen Margaret, however arrogant, was at least leading a human army. Still, she reflected uneasily, those Scots could kill her just as dead.

With Rus jumping excitedly beside her, she made her way to where Welly was standing by the horses. Everyone was too intent on his own fears and preparations to bother avoiding a young magic worker and her mutant dog. She hardly noticed the others, but smiled when she saw Welly. He looked impressively martial in his metal-studded armor. But already there was a sheen of sweat on his face, and one plump hand was fidgeting with the horsehead hilt of his own Eldritch sword.

Over the steady howling of wind, horses neighed, men shouted orders, and metal clattered on metal as soldiers swung into saddles and hurried to their positions. The cold air smelled of horse, leather, and sweat.

"Further east!" Arthur shouted to Otto, as a groom brought up the king's gray horse. "Keep to the high ground but move further east. The drop-off on the Wall's far side is too steep here. We can't risk being driven against it."

The king swung onto his horse, and Welly, Heather, and others did the same. Already John Wesley, seated proudly on his shaggy brown mare, had raised the Pendragon banner. It snapped above them in the sharp, icy air.

With Arthur and his standard in the lead, the king's troop pulled out. Merlin rode up beside Heather and Welly. "Stick with me," he said over the din of horses and men, "and stay uphill from the king."

To the blare of horns and roll of drums, the army began flowing eastward. Heather looked ahead at the enemy advancing to the eerie wail of bagpipes. They were closer now but not close enough to pick out individuals. She wondered if the smudge of their own army looked as large and daunting to the Scots. There were a lot of people on both sides. Earl was right. Once they had finished fighting, no matter who won, there'd be a lot of people dead.

She squelched the thought and, like many others, strained for a glimpse of Queen Margaret. Riding beside his friend, Welly pointed. "There she is, on that big red horse. Guess that's her banner in front."

Heather kept her eyes on that distant figure. Even from so far away, she could see the queen's flaming red hair. The banner was a splash of red on gold, but she couldn't make out the device.

Suddenly Merlin was beside them, working his black mare like a sheepdog to cut them off. "Higher. We don't want to get swept up in the charge." Rus yapped eagerly, and Heather shot him a hushing look.

Both armies slowed, seeking favorable positions. Arthur held the north ridge while across a shallow swale, still scarred by Roman ditches, the Scots took a lower swell of ground.

Heather could see the queen better now. She looked young, not the brutish veteran everyone seemed to have expected. The banner was clearly a rearing red lion blazoned on gold.

Merlin maneuvered his horse between them. "When the charge is sounded, head for those rocks." Welly opened his mouth to protest, but Merlin cut him short. "No, I'm not asking you to hide. Look, this is the plan."

After his instructions, Heather felt twice as scared as before. "I don't know if I can do that, Earl. I've never tried to. . . ."

A challenging horn brayed over the hills and was answered by another across the swale. Voices rose in growling shouts, and like water bursting from dams, the two armies poured toward each other, yelling and brandishing weapons.

"There," Merlin shouted as the three galloped toward the rocks. "Arthur's holding back at first, directing things from that knoll. He'll join in later. And see, there's Margaret doing the same. You can always find her by the banner. Now, Heather, the queen's horse!"

But Heather was already looking at the horse, a big red stallion. His ears pricked forward eagerly, and his mane bristled along the proud arched neck. He snorted and pawed the earth. He had known many battles and would wait for command, but not patiently. He wanted to run with his fellows, to carry his mistress into the exciting chaos, to strike with his hooves at any who faced him.

"Closer!" Heather's voice was strained. Welly, his hand on her bridle, had been steadily leading her. The three were now east of the battle. On a rise above them and to their west, were the queen and her guard. The shallow valley vibrated with sound, the sound of screaming horses and men and of weapons clashing on armor.

"Now, Heather," Merlin urged. "Now!"

Heather followed the paths she'd forged, reaching into the red horse's eager, battle-hungry mind. *This is the way. Now is the command. The only way, the only time to join the battle. This way. Now!*

The queen's horse screamed and bolted sideways, his rider struggling to stay on his back. Heather stared at the joyous, tossing head. *Yes, that's right, this way, faster! Let no one stop you. This is the way, the only way to battle.*

The horse veered east and then plunged down the slope. Confused, the queen's guard watched a moment, then, seeing her danger, they prodded their horses after her.

Suddenly a mounted warrior sprang out of nowhere in front of the guard, a stout young man waving a fabulous sword. Then there were others, many others, all alike, brandishing identical swords. Alarmed, the soldiers pulled out their own weapons.

The young warriors laughed, sun glinting off their spectacles. Eerily they laughed as one, and as one they turned and rode on ahead, surrounding the queen and her run-away mount.

Now at the feet of the pursuers, warhounds appeared, dozens of them, all hideous. With two heads each, they snapped and snarled, and the guards' horses plunged in terror.

Surrounded by unearthly dogs and warriors, the queen's horse continued its mad flight behind enemy lines. Closer and closer they drew to the gold and black banner of Arthur Pendragon.

The battle slowly faltered. "They've captured Margaret!" came the word. "Arthur's taken the queen!" Fighting slowed under a weight of confusion, and in places the Scottish line wavered and broke.

On the hillside, Queen Margaret had given up trying to control her horse, or turn it back from its insane flight. She cared now only to stay on with dignity, but that had nearly been shaken by the sudden appearance of the strange, identical warriors and their horrid two-headed hounds. Surrounded, she could scarcely see where this mad charge was taking her. Then her eye caught a flutter of black blazoned with a snarling gold dragon.

Suddenly the host around her shimmered and shrank— into one boy and a single grotesque dog. At her other side rode two more warriors. No, these two were hardly more than children, a wispy-haired girl and a pale, scrawny boy. Confusion and indignation threatened to choke her. Then she looked ahead.

A tall, fair man sat astride a stallion as large as her own. He took off his helmet, and golden hair glinted in the pale sun. His smile was broad but bewildered. "Your Majesty, to what do I owe this honor?"

She stared at him in silent anger, but the thin boy beside her spoke up. "Her Majesty, Queen Margaret, is here to discuss a truce and an alliance."

She turned savagely on the youth. "I'm here to do nothing of the sort!"

"Oh, yes, you are, Your Majesty," he said softly. "What other choice have you?"

From his horse, Arthur smiled in comprehension and signaled to his trumpeter to sound a blast. As the echoes faded, the skirmishing below lessened.

The king stood in his stirrups, his voice booming over the battlefield. "I, Arthur Pendragon, hold Margaret, Queen of Scots as my . . . guest. To assure her safety and yours, let all hostilities between our two forces cease."

"Your Majesty." Arthur turned to the Queen as a babble of voices broke out below. "Let us and some of our aides retire to a quieter spot. It seems we have a good deal to discuss."

Margaret's face had turned an angry red, almost the shade of her hair. But her voice was like ice. "Am I to have aides at this 'talk' as well?"

"Certainly. Give us the names, and we will send for them."

Arthur directed their horses up the hillside toward scattered rocky ruins. Behind them, Heather suddenly swayed in her saddle. Merlin quickly reached over and steadied her.

"Oh Earl," she said weakly. "I feel as if I've been flayed on the inside."

"It will pass. But need I say, you did splendidly?"

"You certainly did, Heather," Welly chimed in. "But I almost forgot to look ferocious when those copies popped up, all looking as terrified as I did. There were an awful lot of me."

Merlin chuckled. "And all played their parts beautifully. So did Rus. I threw him in at the last minute. It was a pretty good touch though, wasn't it?"

"Brilliant," Welly agreed. "One of him is enough for most folks. But let's catch up with the others."

Higher on the slope, a small assembly was dismounting and finding seats among the weed-choked ruins. The red-haired queen sat by herself, tall and erect, with a face as cold and stony as the wall on which she sat. However, when Heather, Welly, and Merlin rode up, her face kindled with anger.

"So, now this travesty of a council is to be joined by children? I won't have it!"

"Madam," Arthur said calmly. "These 'children' not only persuaded you to join us, they battled their way through great evil to fetch me out of Avalon. Their swords are Eldritch, and their rights unquestioned."

The queen jumped angrily to her feet. "Avalon and Eldritch swords, bah! Maybe you can delude your simple hill folk with such fancies, but not me! I'll talk to you about armies and land—I have no choice. But I will not talk about fairy tales!"

Arthur took an angry breath, but Merlin held up his hand. Dismounting wearily, he faced the queen. "Your Majesty, may I point out that a woman whose horse has been called from her by the power of magic and whose guard has been threatened by spectral warriors, is hardly in a position to question fairy tales."

The queen's sputtering reply was cut short by the arrival of four of her lieutenants. Looking confused, angry, and worried, they reluctantly turned over their swords and joined their queen.

The king nodded at the newcomers. "Thank you for joining us gentlemen. Now let us begin. We should have a neutral mediator, but as none is available, I suggest that Merlin begin the discussion. The idea for these talks was, I believe, his."

Queen Margaret raised an eyebrow when the same skinny boy stood up. This was the fabled Merlin? Nonsense. Even in fairy tales he was an old graybeard. Still, there were all those phantom warriors. . . .

"Your Majesties," Merlin bowed to each, "and nobles of Scotland and the North. This truce provides an opportunity to reevaluate our situation." The Scottish generals snorted, but Merlin ignored them. "We have below us the fighting forces of all northern Britain. Between us we've achieved more unity than this island has seen in five hundred years. But if this battle continues, a chance for greater unity is shattered. Both armies are strong; there would be no easy victory." This time generals on both sides snorted. "No matter who won, hatreds would last for generations, and the fighting forces of these lands would be devastated. Half, maybe more, of our warriors would die."

"That's the hazards of war, boy," one of the Scotsmen called out. Merlin could see grizzled veterans on his own side nod in agreement.

"Perhaps you are right. Perhaps Britain should remain a pack of barbaric states snarling and biting at each other. Perhaps we don't want the peace, prosperity, and unity these lands once knew. If so, we should continue this battle and let the carrion eaters claim victory.

"But even were that our goal, we would not enjoy it long. Because there is another form of unity alive in these islands, a unity of evil. You all know mutants have been crossing the diminished Channel from the Continent, but these are not aimless destroyers. They have found a leader, someone with power enough to turn them to her will. And her will is to conquer Britain, all of Britain, for herself."

Uneasy muttering broke out in the assembly.

"Look at the start she has made. Five shires already are in her hands! And her armies number not only conscripts and foreign muties but creatures from another world. Morgan is an enchantress." Angry scoffing sounds. "This is no fairy tale! It is as real as the little magics emerging around your own lands." He looked around at the uneasy nods. "Magic is returning, and there is none who can wield it for greater evil than Morgan La Fay.

"Every day that we fight among ourselves, she grows stronger. Every loss we suffer is one less obstacle for her. And what can stem her conquest of this divided island if we are busy licking our self-inflicted wounds?

"But if, instead, we unite, we could move south and spread our unity. The size of our combined forces would convince many to join rather than resist us. And when, in time, we faced the real enemy, we might hope for the strength to triumph."

Merlin sat down to scattered cheers from both sides. A black-bearded Scotsman spoke up. "You are suggesting we unite our two armies, but under whose command? We're not buying your claims that this golden puppy is High King of Britain."

Several Cumbrians jumped up angrily. Merlin stood, raising his staff. "The command would be a joint one, the King of Cumbria and Queen of Scotland sharing equally, along with a council of their choosing."

The Scottish queen now jumped to her feet. "If you are asking me to share command with this arrogant young play-actor. . . ."

Arthur, purpling with rage, stood as well. "Madam, if you think I want to share anything with an uncouth, snarling fell bitch like yourself. . . ."

Merlin stomped his staff against the ground, producing a shower of purple sparks. "Shut up, Your Majesties! I am not asking that you like each other, only that you lead your armies away from self-destruction to possible victory. Surely both you youngsters are mature enough for that!"

"Well!" Margaret said indignantly. "You're hardly the one to talk, you nasty little beardless brat!"

Arthur laughed gustily. "Madam, that nasty little beardless brat is several thousand years your senior. But I admit, age hasn't made his meddling any easier to take—particularly when he's right."

Arthur turned and jumped onto a wall. "All right. I accept the proposal." He looked coldly at the queen. "My army is as ready and anxious for battle as yours. But we are even more anxious for lasting victory. If that can best be found by uniting forces and moving south, then let us do so. I will share command with Scotland's queen, but I ask that our advisers do their utmost to keep us out of each other's way!"

The queen rose with disdainful dignity. "I, too, accept the proposal. The forces of Scotland will gladly conquer any southlands laid before us. And if to do so I must accept joint command, I will. But on one point I agree with this pale upstart. Councillors be warned—the less we two have to do with each other, the better!"

Heated discussion began over the details of the alliance. Heather and Welly joined Merlin where he sat by himself, looking tired and depressed.

"What are you so down for?" Welly asked. "That was a stupendous speech. It really seemed to do the trick."

Merlin smiled wanly. "A bit flowery, I'm afraid, but it worked. No, what worries me is that the 'beardless brat' line could rankle me so. Last time I was this age, it took me forever to grow a beard, and that drove me absolutely crazy. Now my body's doing the same thing again. You'd think I'd have the sense not to let it bother me. But it does! I guess it just shows that the age shifting was complete. I'm a teenager again, inside and out. What an ordeal!"

The following evening, the leadership of both armies joined for dinner. It began as an awkwardly stiff affair, but after the barley beer made several rounds, a semblance of camaraderie spread through the group. Arthur and Margaret sat on opposite sides of the fire sharing good-humored chatter with those around them but having nothing but glowers for each other.

After Scotish pipers had screeched for a while, Kyle launched nervously into a newborn song of his own. He had worked on it frantically all day, trying to make all participants in the recent battle sound equally dignified and brave. He finally avoided the problem of whom to glorify most by playing up the magic element instead.

Afterward, when less tuneful songs were being belted out by the diners, Heather slipped over to the harpist.

"Kyle, that song was terrific." She smiled wryly. "But I couldn't help noticing how much you made use of magic and all. I thought you hated it."

"One can't *hate* magic any more than one can hate fire. But that doesn't mean I want nice people getting hurt by it."

"If you're going to lecture . . ."

"I'm not. I'm a harper, and magic is a natural for songs

and stories. But did you like the way the song showed you?"

"I . . . well, it wasn't anything like me—a cool, magical heroine, ha! But you've told me often enough how an artist has to mold raw mud into something lovely."

"Yes. But the hearers don't see the trick. If it's artfully done, they take it for truth. Soon they'll see you not as Heather McKenna but as that cool, magical heroine. They'll leave a wide space around you just as they do with Merlin. They'll be afraid if your hem brushes against them. Think, Heather, is that what you want? Because, slowly, that is what you are choosing."

Heather paled and turned away. Kyle had jabbed into her deepest fears. She didn't want to make that choice, not yet. She needed time to think, to decide!

Just then Otto bawled something and swayed drunkenly to his feet. With relief, Heather turned toward the commotion.

"A toast!" he repeated. "To the alliance of King Arthur and Queen Margaret!"

A portly Scot jumped up as well. "Aye. An alliance started on a battlefield may end in a marriage bed!"

Otto laughed and swung his mug on high. "Now, that's diplomacy. I'll drink to that!"

"You shall not!" Margaret shrieked and jumped up, flinging her mug into the fire. "None of you shall, or I march out of here tonight! I've had enough of my 'advisers' trying to marry me off to any princeling who doesn't fall off his horse. I am queen. And I am not sharing my throne with any arrogant English madman. The next person who suggests I do gets my sword through his throat!"

Arthur was on his feet now, glaring across the fire at her and the whole assembly. "Save your sword for your own men, Queen. The next man of mine who so much as thinks of mating me with an uncouth wild-woman will feel my own blade. Now, all of you, do this lady and I make ourselves clear on this point?"

The shocked mumbling was broken into by the sound of

horsemen on the hillside above. Moments later one of Arthur's guards rode up and, dismounting, hastily bowed to the king.

"Your Majesty, there's a man here with a message from the Duke of Cheshire. He's sought you in Keswick, Carlisle, and now here. Will you see him?"

"I will. Anything would be preferable to the insanity I've just been hearing."

The guard motioned into the darkness. A spent horse stumbled forward, and a man dismounted and walked wearily toward the king. He bowed and looked up at Arthur with a moment's awe. Then, composing himself, he stammered, "You are Arthur Pendragon?"

"I am."

"Then, Sire, I have a most urgent message for you from His Grace, Geoffrey, Duke of Cheshire."

"Deliver it then. These are allies, we have no secrets."

The young messenger straightened himself and unrolled the parchment clutched in his hand. " 'To Arthur Pendragon, High King of Cumbria and Carlisle, from Geoffrey, the third of that name, Duke of Cheshire.

" 'Sire, having heard much of your prowess, both in olden times and of late, and having heard that you seek alliances among the shires, let me extend the offer of such. We are in dire need. Chester, our chief city, has for weeks been laid siege to by the armies of Manchester. Our supplies grow short, but the enemy shows no sign of tiring. We are an ancient and proud people, but we would rather lay our allegiance at the feet of one known for his openness than have it wrested from us by the greedy hands of old enemies. In hopes that soon I may offer you my gratitude in person, I am yours, Geoffrey III, Duke of Cheshire.' "

"Thank you, young man," Arthur said to the courier. "Someone fetch him food and drink." He turned to the others. "What do you say, Your Majesty? We must try this alliance out somewhere."

The queen smiled coldly across the fire. "I say we march to Chester."

Cheers broke out, and cries of "To Chester, to Chester!" Quietly Arthur turned to Merlin. "I'd ask a prophecy if you'd give it, old wizard. But have you at least some feeling on this plan? Is it right that we march to Chester?"

Standing beside Merlin, Heather looked at her friend anxiously as his face creased with pain. His voice was low and strained. "It is right, and it is wrong. But it is the way you must go. I know nothing more."

"Well, that's enough for me," Arthur said, turning back to the others.

Merlin gazed at Heather, his eyes blank with anguish. "No, it is not enough! I should be able to tell him more."

She reached for his hand, but there was nothing comforting she could think to say. Above them in the dark, she felt the passage of a lone night bird. It soared on winds of cold foreboding. Fear and terrible emptiness slid beneath its wings. She shivered and clutched the wizard's hand tighter in her own.

nine

The Road to War

When the armies marched south from the Wall, it was with Dragon and Lion banners fluttering in the lead. John Wesley had struck up a friendship with the young Scot who carried Margaret's standard, and the two rode close abreast.

The farther south they moved, the grimmer the landscape became. Heather was surprised at the desolation. Since only London had been bombed during the Devastation, she'd assumed that most old cities would not look greatly shattered. But with massive deaths from cold, radiation, and plague, their social and economic order had quickly collapsed. The few survivors had fled, and the once great cities had fallen into ruins. They were inhabited now only by scavengers and bands of mutants.

Between these ruins were scattered farms and small settlements from which supplies were taken for the advancing army. But when their route took them past the hollow cities, an oppressive silence fell over the company, as though a cloud of dead dreams still hung about the ruins.

The roads they followed were straight and wide, but under the weeds, the pavement was cracked. Overpasses were collapsed, and tall metal lightposts sprawled beside the roads like dead giants. On every side, skeletons of buildings and smokestacks stood silhouetted against the dust-gray sky.

Of all those in the southward-marching army, the king's wizard seemed most deeply sunk in gloom. Whenever Heather tried to talk to him, he muttered something about roads cycling back and continued staring at the dead landscape.

By the time they crossed the Cheshire border, Merlin's tension was so apparent, no one rode anywhere near him. Even Heather and Welly were afraid to speak to him for fear he might shatter like a figure of glass. Instead they rode with Kyle or trotted forward to exchange words with John Wesley.

After many long, gray days, the vanguard finally climbed a low rise and saw, in a glinting bend of the River Dee, the ancient walled town of Chester. The besieging army from Manchester clustered like ants outside the wall. But warned of the North's coming, they were already redeploying their forces.

Margaret and Arthur consulted briefly with their generals, and word was given to fan out along a low ridge. Turning her eyes from the deployment, Heather glanced to where Merlin sat, hunched dejectedly on his horse. Appalled at how ill he looked, she spurred her horse over to him.

"Earl, I don't want to disturb you, but you really don't look well. Maybe you should just stay back here. They probably won't need magic in this one."

He shuddered and glanced at her as if suddenly coming awake. "It's wrong! Every step we take and every road I see is wrong. They lead in huge circles. We ride past ruins on our way to war. There'll be little wars, then bigger wars, until we build cities of our own and blast them into ruins to crawl past once more. There must be somewhere to turn aside, but I can't see it!"

He cried that last with such despair that those nearby

sketched hand signs against evil and moved away. "Earl," Heather said, "if you think we're going to lose this battle. . . ."

"No! No, it's two separate things. Both connected though . . . somehow. But I can't see either very well—the long-term doom or the short-term battles. With the battle at the Wall, I was just fumbling in the dark. It seemed to work, but it led us here. And what will happen today? Who will die, and where will it lead us? A wizard worth the name should be able to tell. But without the new magic or even the use of my old tools, how can I?

"And then there's the big battle, the one with Morgan: It's coming, it lies before us as surely as tomorrow's dawn. But what is she planning, what is her strength? Have we any hope of defeating her? If we don't, then all my brooding about mankind's future is just empty thought. The future she'll bring . . . servitude, torture, and evil. Better that the Devastation had wiped the human race out entirely and cleansed this planet than left us to drown in that!"

His head hung over his horse's bowed neck. Then he began shaking with silent laughter. "I'm sorry, Heather. I really do sound like a demented old wizard. To answer the question that I think you asked somewhere back there: No, I won't sit it out. I may be useless as a prophet, but I can still wield a sword."

Heather had understood only part of his words, but the suffering behind them was clear. She almost wished that he was plain Earl Bedwas again. If magic and its responsibilities could eat at a person, a person she cared for, like some terrible disease, then how could anyone want it?

Suddenly horns blared. Movement erupted around her, and Heather instantly lost sight of any military tactics. She concentrated on keeping astride her horse as it pounded over the plain, on watching where her crazy dog was getting to, and on keeping close to the king's standard. She hoped that as long as she thought of mechanical things, she'd forget to be afraid. She was wrong.

Nearby, Welly employed his own and, he discovered,

largely useless device for ignoring fear. He watched patterns unfold from mental plans to the actual battlefield. The king's and queen's guards had pulled up on a rise, while below, the front line formed into a shield-protected wedge to drive through the Manchester line. The cavalry was taking positions on the flanks waiting to trap the enemy in tightening pincers, while the mounted troops around their leaders fidgeted in anticipation of their own final drive through the center.

Suddenly right around them, all became noise and chaos. Nothing was as it should be. Welly and Heather craned their necks to the right, looking for the cause of the turmoil. Then it was all too clear.

A troop fresh from Manchester had come upon the battle and attacked the Northern forces from the rear. Like a spear, they were driving toward the banners of the two war leaders. Their plan was simple and obvious: Kill or capture those two, and the Northern attack would crumble.

The sudden disturbance shocked Merlin out of his lethargy. With grim determination, he pulled out his own gleaming Eldritch sword and sent power flickering along its blade so that it slashed with strength far beyond his own. But the enemy seemed everywhere. No sooner had one fallen than another took its place.

In the center of it all, Queen Margaret, her hair flying about her like flame, cast her spear at one foeman, then drew her sword. Beside her, Arthur's great sword swung through the air, sun glinting off its ancient blade. It slashed down into an attacker, spraying the air with blood. He raised his sword again when suddenly the gray stallion rose screaming onto his hind feet, a deep gash from a war axe streaming blood down his neck. The horse pawed the air then tumbled over, throwing the king to the ground. Dazed, Arthur struggled to his knees as a bloody axe cleaved the air toward him. The axeman's face, snarling in victory, suddenly contorted as the queen's sword drove deep between his ribs.

Warrior and axe thudded to the bloodied earth, and Arthur staggered to his feet beside Margaret's horse. She reached down, and he swung onto the saddle behind her.

Several horse-lengths away, Merlin watched this scene with horror as he automatically fought off attackers with his own sword. Now he wrenched himself away and plunged through the skirmishing warriors to defend his king.

But Arthur and Margaret were doing a capable job of defending themselves, each wielding a sword on a different side of the great red horse. Suddenly Merlin heard an odd cry behind him, high like a young bird's. He spun around to see John Wesley clutching the king's banner, his face blank with surprise as he looked down at the quivering spearshaft protruding from his chest. Slowly his hands slid down the pole, and the boy toppled sideways off his horse.

"No!" Merlin roared. From the tip of his sword, he shot a bolt of flame that incinerated the spearman. Before the ashes had drifted to the ground, Merlin was off his horse holding the dead boy in his arms.

Welly, fighting nearby, had heard Merlin's shout and turned to see the Dragon standard waver and slide downward along the now riderless horse. Driving his horse toward it, Welly reached out and grabbed the pole. Awkwardly he wielded his sword with one hand while clutching the standard with the other.

Battle tides surged back and forth over plain and hill. Below, the Northern wedge finally broke through the Manchester line and scattered the besieging forces. When they saw their main army routed, the reinforcements wavered, then called a retreat. Northerners cheered their departure, vengefully pursuing stragglers.

When relative calm had returned to the battlefield, Heather looked down at her sword to see it red and sticky. Sick horror rose in her throat and she hastily dismounted to wipe the blade on the grass. Distrusting her wobbly legs, she mounted again and looked over the battlefield.

On a hillside littered with dead and dying, she saw Merlin's black horse riderless and alone. Fear sliced through her like a spear. She spurred her horse to a gallop. As she neared, Welly, having turned in the standard, rode up as well.

Heather felt faint with relief when she saw Merlin kneeling, apparently unharmed, but her joy shriveled at the sight of what he held in his arms. She and Welly dismounted.

"He died," their friend whispered. "He was nine years old, and he died."

"He died nobly," Welly said, his own voice strained and tearful.

"Oh, yes, nobly!" Merlin laughed bitterly. "That makes it all right then. He died nobly clutching the standard of the king. And you nobly saved it from being trampled in his blood, and Kyle the harper will compose a ballad about how noble we all were and how tragically and nobly the crippled boy from Devon died, and we'll all feel sad and somehow better about it." The bitterness in his voice was as sharp as a sword.

Angry now, Welly snapped, "And I suppose you'd rather I'd let the standard fall?"

"No! No, I'd rather you'd never had to save it. I'd rather this whole bloody waste had never happened!"

"But, Earl," Welly objected, "you said we had to unify the country and face Morgan. . . ."

"I know. And we do. That *is* right. But something is wrong too, very wrong. If only I could see what!" He laid the limp form gently on the ground. "If I could have seen this battle, if I could have seen the relief column from Manchester, then this boy wouldn't be lying here now. If I could see further, we'd know what we faced with Morgan; or further still, and maybe I could keep us from plunging down that same long, deadly road. But I can't, I can't see any of it!"

Hesitantly, Heather placed a hand on his shoulder, tears streaming down her own face. "Earl, we loved John Wesley, too. But this isn't your fault. None of it is. You're doing the best you can."

He reached up and grabbed her hand. "No. I am *not* doing that. That's one thing I do know."

The wind froze the tears to her cheeks as Heather looked down at his ashen face and the sad dead boy beside him on the grass. This world, she thought, was harsh enough without the demands of magic. That was an added curse, one no one should have to bear.

The seige of Chester was broken. Duke Geoffrey rode forth from his city to thank the liberating army and its leaders. He invited them to enter as victorious allies on the morrow. The remainder of that day and evening were spent tending to the dead and wounded.

The battlefield was strewn with the bodies of soldiers and horses. They were gathered up, friend and foe alike, and placed in a large, freshly dug grave. A great stone was erected on the raw heaped-up earth, but no writing was placed upon it. The pain was still too fresh to have distilled into words.

The following morning, Duke Geoffrey rode out again and presented to Arthur a rare throwback, a tall white warhorse, to replace the horse fallen in battle. Those who knew Arthur, knew he'd feel nothing could replace his gray. But the king accepted the gift; it was a magnificent animal.

A dawn drizzle had given way to pale sunshine. To the throb of drums and the peal of pipes, the victorious army marched toward the city they had saved. First, under Lion and Dragon banners, rode Queen Margaret, a blaze of red, and King Arthur, hair and sword gleaming gold. Their great horses pranced and tossed their heads. Behind them came their warriors, battered weapons and armor hastily polished and flashing in the sun. People who had poured out of the city for the first time in weeks cheered wildly and strained for a glimpse of their deliverers.

As the host neared the city, Duke Geoffrey proudly pointed out how Chester had strengthened its defenses by pulling down structures that had sprawled beyond its medieval wall. People lined that wall now, cheering, waving, and throwing down bits of cloth and anything bright. Chants of "Arthur" and "Margaret" filled the air as the two rode under the gate. The streets were crowded with jubilant people, who stood amid a crazy mixture of buildings: medieval half-timber,

Georgian stone, and twentieth-century concrete, all patched with rubble for modern utility.

Triumphantly they rode on, finally clattering into the duke's ancient castle, built into the city's south wall. Soldiers found welcome and lodging among celebrating townfolk, but the king and queen and their closest followers were lodged in the castle. That night they dined as royally as the town's scanty provisions, augmented just that day, would permit.

It was a noisy feast, noisy with the relief people feel after having lived through a victorious battle. In a smoky, torch-lit hall, dancers whirled while Kyle and other musicians played pipe, harp, and drum. Heroic events of the previous day were already elaborating into legend.

Seated apart at one corner of the king's table, Merlin alone seemed immune to the jollity. Silently he picked at the food before him or stared desolately into his cup of ale. The cup was a simple unadorned one, beaten from some salvaged metal. With the noise and torchsmoke swirling around him, he stared unheeding into the cup's brown depths.

Foamy bubbles and shapes were there. Shapes of warriors marching towards a city, a walled city by a river, besieged by enemies. The warriors spread out to attack, and as they did so an unguessed-at enemy drove toward them like a spear, taking them by surprise. Surprise as the troops rallied around their king and queen. Surprise on the face of a young boy clutching at a banner, dying with a spear thrust through his chest.

Merlin clenched his hand around the cup. It felt wider now, polished silver carved with intricate designs. In its depths, the boy's face still held surprise, eternal dying surprise. But there should have been no surprise! He should have known. He should have known!

Leaping up, Merlin hurled the cup across the room. In sudden silence, everyone turned toward him. Slowly his vision cleared, and he looked down the table at the king. "Arthur, help me!"

"Tell me how."

In the crowded, breathless room, there might have been only these two.

"Arthur, I must know what happened to my things after . . . I disappeared."

"After Nimue took you from Caerleon?"

"Yes."

The young man sat back and stared, unseeing, across the room, stared back through centuries into another life. "We didn't know what had happened to you," he said slowly. "They said Nimue had enchanted you, had entombed you in some mountain. But we didn't know where. If you'd been dead somewhere, we would have buried your things with you. But . . . what are you thinking about in particular?"

"My silver bowl."

"The carved one that hung at your belt?"

Merlin nodded, and again the king thought. "I think I told Bedevere, my squire, to take care of all those things. I don't remember what happened to the bowl particularly. Since it was silver, I imagine it was treated as part of the royal treasury."

"And what would have happened to it?"

"I don't know. It could have been kept in the storeroom at Caerleon, or moved on to Camelot, or I suppose it could eventually have been given out as a reward to some loyal vassal, or maybe even melted down for coinage. I really, don't know, Merlin, but obviously it's important."

"Yes, it is." He nodded at the king. "If you will excuse me, Sire, I need to think."

Arthur nodded back, and Merlin left the room. The others in the room were silent in awe, as if a window had just opened onto an ancient mythical past.

Looking around, Arthur sensed the mood. Sighing, he closed that window. "Now, ladies and gentlemen, to the concerns of our own time. Let us have a toast. A toast to Duke Geoffrey of Cheshire and his welcoming city and to Queen Margaret of Scotland and her most welcome sword."

The people in the room cheered and raised their cups. Their king was back.

After the banquet, Heather was shown to the room she would share with several ladies of Cheshire's court. They were eager to know about Arthur, about the strange, frightening Merlin, and about beautiful Queen Margaret. Restlessly, Heather chatted with them a while, but as soon as she could, she slipped a cape over her borrowed dressing gown and said she had to say goodnight to someone. Rus, told to remain behind, woefully obeyed.

She found Merlin on the battlements. There was no mistaking his thin, gangly figure or the pale smudge of his face in the darkness. Above them, the moon, through the high dust, cast misty light on the Welsh mountains rolling darkly to the southwest.

He turned as he heard her approach, but said nothing.

"Earl, what are you going to do?"

"Go find it."

"The bowl? But Arthur said it might be anywhere or even melted down by now."

"I know. But I have to try. Without it, I'm of no use to him or anyone."

"That's silly. That trick with Margaret. . . ."

"Yes, but it was just that, a trick, and one that counted on luck. Yesterday, Arthur won without tricks, but the luck ran out for John Wesley, didn't it? I should have been able to foresee that."

"Earl, you couldn't. . . ."

"Heather, I could have. I've been so submerged in worry over the new magic and the far future that I've neglected the present, and that's our only sure link to the future. What happens if Arthur is defeated in our next battle? What happens to the future then? At the stone circle, you had a vision. You saw a battlefield strewn with Arthur's warriors. When is that a possibility? Will it come after meeting Morgan? That is the big confrontation, and she knows it's coming as well as we do. She'll be planning for it—something diabolical, no doubt—and I want to know what. That Bowl of Seeing is the only way I know to find out. It may not work in this world; it may not even still exist. But I've got to try something!"

"So where will you go?" Heather asked after a moment.

"To Caerleon first. Arthur moved his court around a good deal, but that was where we were when Nimue. . . ."

"I know. You don't have to talk about it."

"No, but oddly I want to. Tonight raked up all those memories. It's hard to believe a wise old wizard could have been so blind. But Morgan wanted me out of the way, and she had learned my weakness. All my years of magic had cut me off from simple human caring. I was bitterly lonely, and Nimue filled that loneliness. With Morgan's guidance, she learned enough of my secrets to trap me in my own enchantments."

He sighed quietly, then turned and looked at Heather. "I know what Kyle's been saying to you, Heather, and he's right. I haven't wanted to admit it. I'd hoped that this time my life could be different, that I could let myself be close to people. I was so happy when I thought that you and I could . . . share the working of magic. But it's no good. Having this power and letting it grow controls your life. It cuts you off. People come to fear or hate you. I have no right to lead you away from a normal life into that."

"Earl, you're not. . . . It's just that. . . . Oh, I don't know. I don't know what to think."

"Yes you do. You know I'm right. You've been a good friend, and that's more than I should have hoped for. But I'm fooling myself to think there is any choice. This road I must go alone."

The silence stretched on and on. There was so much Heather wanted to say. Yet her mind churned with confused thoughts which she seemed powerless to mold into words.

On the battlefield, she'd felt part of herself crumble when she'd thought Earl had been killed. She ought to tell him now she'd go with him, help him, share the exile of power. But her mind recoiled from that. She had a whole life to lead. Could she bear to lead it like that—shunned, feared, self-tormented as he was? The taste she'd had of that was chilling enough.

Choked by fear and indecision, she said nothing.

At last Merlin broke the silence. "I'll leave tonight. Arthur will know I have to go, but I'd rather not face any more leave-taking. If . . . when I find the bowl or learn what became of it, I'll return. Tell him that for me, will you?"

She nodded bleakly.

"And Heather. . . ."

"Yes?"

"No, nothing. Yes, maybe there is something. I'll be taking the route past your family's home in Brecon. Do you want me to stop with any message?"

"Oh." She looked away. "Yes, I suppose so. You know my mother and I haven't had much to do with each other since she remarried. She'd rather produce heirs for Lord Brecon than bother with her homely firstborn. But still . . . she is my mother. If you stop, let her know I'm all right. At least they should give you a warm meal and a bed. Knowing my stepfather, he wouldn't offend anyone important."

She tried to think furious thoughts about her uncaring family, but her mind was too numb for real emotions of any sort.

Merlin looked down at her, his own face tight against unspoken feelings. "I'll try to stop at Brecon, then. Good-bye, Heather."

"Good-bye." He started to turn. "Earl. . . ."

"Yes?"

"I. . . . Please come back."

He smiled tautly. "I'll try."

As he walked away, the words she wanted to cry after him fell silently down inside her. She leaned against the parapet, wishing she could be as cold and hard and unheeding as the stones.

ten

In Quest of Vision

It was several hours before dawn when Merlin rode his horse down to the city's main gate. The guards halted him, then seeing who it was, blanched and hurried to open the gate. Merlin smiled wryly. The reputation of the king's wizard must have spread rapidly. The guards probably thought that if they questioned his doings, he'd turn them to stone or disintegrate their guardhouse.

The great gate creaked open, and the lone figure on a black horse rode out, hoofbeats echoing hollowly in the cold and silence.

The hazy moon was near to setting in the west. He rode toward it along the dark, lonely road, his thoughts equally dark and lonely. It had been right, what he had said to Heather, but he felt as if he'd just torn out a part of himself and left it on the walls of Chester. His had been a false hope, he knew, but it had sustained him these past two years. Now he felt empty.

The sky grayed toward dawn, and he tried turning his thoughts ahead. As he passed the first dragon-tooth peak of Welsh mountains, his mind told him he was coming home. But his heart did not. Too much had changed.

The mountains of his Wales had been green and fair, clothed in forest and in rich grazing land. Now the rocky slopes were bare of all but dry, gray grass. A few trees huddled in the valleys where rivers fell in wild tumult over rocks, unsoftened by fern and moss.

He passed abandoned farms and villages and an occasional inhabited one, where he stopped for provisions. He traded for Arthur's newly minted coins or more often for news from the outside world. These rugged folk had little dealings with the world beyond their mountains, but they were always hungry for news and tales that could be repeated around an evening's fire.

The wizard concealed his name, calling himself Earl Bedwas, a traveler from King Arthur's court. But though hospitality was always extended, at night he chose to camp by the wayside. He had no wish to depend again on human companionship. Not that he found his own very cheerful, but it was less demanding. And he knew he had nothing to fear from brigands or muties. His few encounters of that sort ended in a flash of power that sent his assailants fleeing back into the rocks and hills.

One morning, Merlin rolled from his blankets to find that instead of frost there was a light dusting of snow. Not unusual for July, but it depressed him. He wanted the wildflowers and chorusing birds of those ancient mornings. Looking up he wished for a lightly blue sky, a sky with honest clouds, not atmospheric veils of soot and dust. He sighed. This world, he knew, was slowly improving, but it would never be the same. All that seemed the same were the ways of people and his pain in dealing with them.

Thoroughly dejected, he walked to his saddlebags, near where his mare was cropping at the short grass, and fumbled around for a chunk of bread and a turnip. Taking these to the stream, he sat on an flat rock and began sluicing the turnip through the cold, clear water. He was just pulling it out, clean and white, when a pale, clawed hand shot from the water and grabbed one end.

Startled, he gripped the turnip and tugged back. For a moment, two pairs of hands struggled back and forth for their prize. Then with a sudden jerk Merlin found himself flying off his rock and into the icy stream. The cold slammed his breath away. Letting go of the turnip, he flailed at the water, slipped under the surface, then gasped and sputtered into the air again.

Through strands of dark hair dripping over his face, he saw another face bobbing before him in the water. Yellow skin drawn tightly over a misshapen skull made huge ears stand out even more. Little close-set eyes stared at him in alarm.

Suddenly the thing lunged, grabbing him around the chest with long, hairy arms. Swallowing water as he sank beneath the surface, Merlin struggled with his captor, managing only to hit his own head against a rock. Vaguely he realized he was being dragged out onto a boulder.

He lay gasping and coughing in the cold air, while a whiny voice muttered beside him. When he'd regained his breath and coughed out most of the water, Merlin sat up dizzily. His assailant squatted near him on the rock, wringing long hands and looking miserable.

"Great Wizard turn me into toad now. Troll nearly drown Great Wizard. Spend rest of life as toad."

"Troll," Merlin said weakly. "You're the troll from the Severn Bridge."

The creature hung its head. "Me was. Me be toad now."

"I'm not turning anyone into toads at present." Merlin shivered in the icy air. "But I've got to get out of these wet clothes."

The troll brightened. "Yes, change clothes. Troll help, like loyal servant. Wizard can turn Troll into toad later."

He scurried like a spider over to Merlin's pack. The horse gave him a sideways stare and shuffled aside. As soon as

Merlin had peeled off his wet clothes, the troll eagerly handed him dry ones. He'd clearly had little experience with clothing and presented everything in the wrong order, but soon Merlin was dressed and relatively warm again.

"Well, Troll," he said as he looked through his other pack, "since you brought the subject up, would you care to share breakfast with me?"

The wispy beard twitched and a broad smile spread above it. Then the creature dropped his eyes. "Me still deserve to be toad."

"Perhaps, but we'll put that off for the moment." Handing him a turnip, Merlin pulled out another for himself. He broke the chunk of bread in half.

Sitting on a rock well away from the stream, Merlin took a bite of his turnip. "Tell me, Troll, what brings you so far from the Severn? You had a pretty good arrangement there, accosting travelers on that bridge. Did you change over from threats to riddles, as I suggested?"

The troll smiled through a huge bite of bread. "Oh yes, me very clever riddling troll. Not big enough to scare folks with 'grind your bones' lines."

"So why did you leave? There're not as many travelers in this part of the world."

The little troll shook his head sadly. "Spot too good. Bigger troll take it. Many folks come from Faerie, from all parts of Faerie, now that things get better here. Little runts like me not keep good spots."

"So you thought you'd find a small, untenanted bridge in Wales?"

His breakfast companion smiled broadly. "Oh, no. Me clever troll. Me remember once meet Great Wizard and friends. Hear they find Avalon and High King. Me go join them. Troll be fierce warrior!"

Merlin laughed. "Yes, I guess you could be, as long as we're not fighting larger bridge trolls." He sobered again. "If you want to find Arthur and . . . the others, I can tell you where they are."

"Great Wizard not go there?"

"No, not now. Maybe later. I need to find something first. Something I lost—a long time ago."

The troll thought a moment, head nodding violently on his spindly neck. "Then Troll stay with Great Wizard and help find lost thing."

Merlin felt a jab of happiness, which he quickly supressed. "No, you should go on. I've no way of knowing if I'll find it or if I'll ever rejoin the others. Besides, it may be dangerous where I'm going."

"Then Great Wizard need Troll for guard. We find lost thing and go back to friends. Nice Lady who feed Troll there, too?"

"Heather. Yes, she and Welly are with Arthur."

"Then must get back safe. Troll help."

Merlin smiled, for the first time in weeks it seemed. "All right, I'll take you on as a traveling companion and guard. We'll forget all about the toad business."

Grinning from ear to huge ear, the troll leaped to his feet and began wadding up the wet clothes and cramming them into a saddlebag. Merlin winced. A traveling companion maybe, but a valet, never.

The Northern armies stayed in and around Chester while wounds were tended and emissaries sent to negotiate a truce with Manchester and perhaps an alliance with York and Lancaster.

Welly, Heather, and the ever eager Rus explored the old walled city. It was the largest settlement they had ever seen, though parts were still uninhabited. The natives took pride in pointing out features of interest, such as the canal and the ancient red stone cathedral. Welly enjoyed these excursions and the training of new recruits, but Heather's thoughts kept drifting off. She spent more and more time on the castle walls looking out to the purple mountains of Wales.

She stood one afternoon on a favorite spot above the spreading branches of Chester's famed oak. Somehow the ancient giant had survived the rigors of the Devastation and continued growing against the castle's sheltering walls. Now in brief summer, its gnarled branches were in leaf. Heather thought that looking down on it was almost like being a bird in flight.

Just then, a real bird flew into view. It was a small hawk and soared with effortless beauty, gliding between herself and the tree below. She reached out her mind and felt the peace and purposefulness of its flight. It circled once then settled itself on a branch below her, calmly folding its wings.

There was sudden motion. A large snake, which had been stretched along the branch, whipped a coil around the bird. The hawk shrieked, flailing with wing and claw. Both creatures fell from the branch, disappearing over a ledge.

Heather gasped, staring in horror at the spot. But she heard or saw nothing more. Suddenly she was buffeted by a cold wind, a wind of fear and terrible certainty. She wanted to scream, to tear the vision from her mind, but it persisted. And, real or illusion, she knew its meaning. Earl had once shown her a picture of a merlin hawk. It had been like this one.

She leaned against the stone parapet as her world swirled around her and suddenly fell into place. If she hadn't been so worried, she would have laughed with relief. Earl was in danger, and in an instant all her uncertainties vanished.

Her power had warned her of Earl's danger, and now perhaps she could help him. Yet this was the same power she had feared would cut her off from the normal world. Well, if it did, then let it. It was Earl that mattered. Until now, she'd been too blind to see that! She'd let him go off alone while she'd crouched, undecided, behind useless shreds of "normality."

She laughed feeling as if great weights had fallen from her. Then, recalling the vision, she hurried down a series of stone steps. In the courtyard, Arthur and Margaret were just riding out to inspect the troops camped beyond the city walls.

"Your Majesties!" Heather called. "Wait a moment, please!" They turned in their saddles and watched her run toward them, braids flying.

"Please," she gasped, "I would like your permission to leave, to go into Wales."

"You, too?" Arthur said. "What is it about Wales that's calling away all my sorcerers?"

"I'm not much of a sorcerer, Your Majesty. But Earl, Merlin, is in danger. I . . . saw it."

The king frowned. "What sort of danger?"

"I don't know. But I know there is danger waiting for him where he least expects it. I have to warn him."

Queen Margaret spoke up. "I should think young Merlin could take care of himself. I've seen a sample or two of his powers."

"Yes, Your Majesty, I'm sure he could if he were prepared. That's why I must warn him."

"Mightn't he have have received a warning as you did?" Arthur asked.

Now it was Heather's turn to frown. "I don't know. But if my help wasn't needed, why did I have the vision?"

The king shook his head. "I don't know, Heather, and I've learned enough not to meddle in affairs of magic. Yes, certainly you may go. Merlin means a great deal to me, adolescent troublemaker as he may be at present." He smiled. "How many should I send with you?"

"Oh, just me, Sire."

"No. Too dangerous."

"Perhaps," the queen suggested, "the young warrior who was so effectively multiplied at our . . . alliance?"

The king nodded. "Welly. Yes, of course. I doubt that he could be kept back anyhow. But wouldn't more be advisable?"

"No, Sire. It's speed, not force, that's needed, I think."

"Well, then, take two of the faster horses, not your hairy barrels-on-legs. That will please Welly, I imagine. And Heather. . . ."

"Yes, Sire?"

"Whether he finds that trinket or not, bring my wizard back to me."

Welly, when she told him, was indeed pleased with the

chance to ride a tall, slimmer horse. He couldn't begin to understand why Heather knew she had to go; but if Earl was in danger, then he, too, was determined to help.

They set out at dawn the next day, Welly and Heather on tall, swift horses with Rus trotting beside them. They took the road they supposed their friend would have taken. Stops at inns and farmhouses confirmed that a tall, pale youth on a black horse had passed that way. Each day Heather urged them on to greater speed. She saw no further portents, but her sense of danger and urgency increased.

For days Merlin and the troll traveled south through Wales. On and off the wizard was annoyed with himself for deriving pleasure from such simple companionship. But since that was the best he could probably ever expect, he decided he might as well enjoy it.

The troll clearly did, sometimes catching fish for their supper and always making a big production of guarding while the wizard slept. Merlin quietly set up additional guarding spells, a wise precaution, he realized, since whenever he woke in the night he found the troll asleep sitting up.

As they neared Brecon, Merlin considered whether to stop at Heather's home. He wasn't anxious to do so since it meant revealing who he was. But whether she admitted it or not, he knew Heather had some feelings for her mother and would like some news of her. Besides, the thought of stopping with Heather's kin made him feel somehow closer to her. Angrily he tried to dismiss the feeling. He had no right to any special closeness with her. Still, he had said he would try to stop.

After asking directions at the Griffin Inn, he took a side road to Lord Brecon's manor. The building had clearly started as a sturdy farmstead with house and barns forming an open courtyard. Over the years it had been added to and fortified into an imposing residence.

It was twilight when, advising his companion to spend the night outside, Merlin rode through the courtyard and up to a heavily barred door. Dismounting, he pounded on the metal-studded wood. A hatch slid open and a squinty-eyed guard peered out.

"I am Earl Bedwas" he announced, "friend of Heather McKenna, daughter to Lady Brecon. I request entry to convey messages between daughter and mother."

The little window slammed shut leaving Merlin to stand impatiently on the stone steps, wondering if, after all, it wouldn't have been better to pass the night with Troll in some quiet ravine. Nonhuman company was usually far less stressful.

He had almost given up hope that his message would be delivered when the door was flung open and torchlight poured out over the steps. Against it a woman stood silhouetted.

"Young sir, welcome. Heather mentioned you in her letters, and I am pleased to meet you. Come in."

He followed the woman inside and down a long stone corridor. The place smelled of age, but even in the hallway woven tapestries hung from the walls. Clearly Lord Brecon was as wealthy as his stepdaughter had said.

They entered a large paneled room. With boastful wastefulness, a fire burned in the stone fireplace, even though it was the middle of summer. In the center of the room stood a carved oak table set with pre-Devastation china. The colorful mix of patterns gleamed softly in light from tallow lamps.

A large, broad-shouldered man stood by the fireplace. He was completely bald and had dark, severe eyes, which lighted in a semblance of welcome as he walked across the room.

"Mr. Bedwas, is it? I understand you are a friend of my stepdaughter's. As such you are welcome. My wife and I were about to dine. We have no other guests this evening and would be honored if you would join us."

"The honor is mine."

Servants appeared from another door and set a third place. Lord Brecon took his seat at the head of the table and motioned the guest to his right. As Merlin sat, he looked carefully for the first time at the woman seated opposite him. He was struck with painful similarities.

Everything about her recalled Heather, but it was as if the mother was the model after which the daughter had been inexpertly copied. Where Heather's hair was dark blond and thin, the mother's was pale gold, full, and wavy. Where Heather's eyes were a muddy gray, the ones across from him glinted like pure sapphires. And Heather's face could only be described as long and thin, while this woman's was slender and delicate. Yet for all that, he couldn't find this person beautiful. She was like an ancient porcelain figurine, perfect in every detail yet cold and hollow inside. There was none of the life and warmth that bubbled up around Heather.

"Well, Earl," Lady Brecon was saying, "I may call you that, mayn't I? Tell us how our dear girl is doing. We've heard from her twice since she left Llandoylan School. Once from Devon saying she'd gone on some important mission with you and another friend, and then a year later from somewhere up in Cumbria saying she'd fallen in with this new King Arthur. I do hope you can tell us a little more."

"Yes, Madam, I will try." Merlin launched into an account of Heather's activities since leaving the Glamorganshire school. It was carefully edited for parental consumption, playing down the hardships and dangers and highlighting the girl's important roles and her place in Arthur's court. He also glossed over the magical elements and their confrontations with Morgan, feeling most people weren't ready to take magic too matter-of-factly.

As he talked, servants brought out a meal that was notably better than most he'd had with Arthur recently. There was rich barley beer as well, and toward the end of the meal, Lord Brecon had a green glass bottle brought out.

"An occasion worth celebrating, I believe. This wine, all the way from Kent, is made from carefully cultured gooseberries. I think you'll like it."

Servants carried out rare glass goblets and poured into them the pale gold contents of the bottle. Merlin sipped at his appreciatively. He hadn't tasted anything calling itself wine in two thousand years. This could hardly compare with the grape wine he had known when Britain was still on the fringes of the Roman world. But it was heady and sweet and had a pleasant fruity taste. He had several glasses while Lord Brecon talked about weather and farming and about their border clashes with the dukedoms of Dyfed and Gwent.

As the man droned on, Merlin began to feel slightly unwell. Maybe it was the heat of the fire-lit room, but he could feel himself breaking into a clammy sweat. The voices around him sounded distant and tinny, and a fuzzy heaviness began settling over him. He wondered if his body was currently too young to deal with that much wine.

It was with relief that he heard Lady Brecon say, "But my dear, I do believe our guest looks tired. I'll have the servants show him to his room."

Gratefully Merlin stood up. Suddenly he was wrenched with a violent dizziness. The room spun like a cartwheel, and the table rose up to meet him. As he smashed to the hard oak, he saw the precious glass goblet roll past him and crash to the floor. That, and a laugh, were the last sounds he heard for some time.

eleven

A Visit Cut Short

When his mind finally struggled to consciousness, it was with the sense that a good deal of time had passed. He seemed to be lying on a thin straw pallet. He could feel its prickliness along the length of his body and the cold rising through it from the stones below.

He tried to sit up. Nothing happened. He tried again, but there wasn't the slightest twitch from any muscle. His head would not turn even a fraction of an inch. He was completely paralyzed. Though his eyes were slightly open, he wasn't able to raise the eyelids further.

Through the fringe of dark lashes, he could see a stone wall glistening with damp. Ten feet from the floor was a small barred window with the grayness of daylight beyond. He could see nothing else.

For several more hours he lay trapped in his cold, motionless body. Only the involuntary muscles of heart and lungs seemed to work at all. He drifted in and out of consciousness until he heard distant voices coming his way.

The sound of a heavy door opening, then the voice of Lord Brecon. "Well, she was certainly right about that drug. Three days now, and he hasn't twitched."

Lady Brecon answered. "I wasn't certain about the dosage when I saw how young he was. But I guess I cut it enough. If we'd killed him, she would have been furious. This should keep him out long enough for your message to reach Cardiff and for Nigel to send someone to fetch him."

Lord Brecon stepped closer, the torchlight gleaming off his bald head. He poked Merlin roughly in the shoulder. There was a slight rattling of chains. "I still don't know why we had to do it this way. A swift blow on the head would have been easier."

"That's what you know! Morgan said he's a powerful wizard, despite his looks. If he could even move a finger or mutter a charm, he'd turn your chains to grass."

"What superstitious rot! You've been taken in by that Morgan woman and her parlor tricks. She's just someone who wants power and found that an alliance with King Nigel is a way to get it."

"Then why do they want this boy so badly?"

"On Nigel's part, a personal vendetta perhaps; and that woman, I believe, wants to use this kid in some power play against your Heather's precious King Arthur. But that's none of our affair, so long as Nigel comes through with the troops and weapons we need against Dyfed."

Lady Brecon moved into Merlin's line of sight. He was struck again by her distorted resemblance to Heather. "Are those chains fastened securely?"

"Afraid of this pipsqueak? I thought you said we didn't even need chains."

"Yes, but who knows how long it'll take those soldiers to get here. If he got loose, he'd turn us into worms."

"Will you shut up about magic! I've put up with your petty witch tricks, but I won't have that woman dazzling you with her blather about 'high powers.' The only power we need is swords and swordsmen."

Footsteps out in the hall and a gruff defferential voice. "Begging you pardon, Your Lordship, but there's a party at the door to see you."

"Ah, maybe they're here," Lady Brecon said. "Now this brat'll be someone else's headache." The pair hurried out of the room, leaving cold and silence behind them.

But when they reached the front door, it was not soldiers from Glamorganshire awaiting them.

"Mother," said a slim girl in a hooded jacket. "May my friend and I stay the night?"

The woman stared at the two with blank astonishment, only slowly pulling herself together. "Heather . . . what . . . ? That is, of course. Come in."

She turned to her husband standing behind her in the shadows. "Look who's here, dear. It's Heather."

The man muttered something and disappeared down the hallway. Lady Brecon led the newcomers to the room with the fireplace.

"My, Heather . . . such a surprise. Whatever brought you here?"

"We're looking for a friend of ours. He was coming this way and said he might stop here. Calling himself Earl Bedwas, maybe. Have you seen him?"

Turning away, the woman took a small log from beside the hearth and threw it into the fire. "Why yes, dear, he was here. About three days ago."

"And where did he go afterwards?"

"I don't know. He didn't say, dear. Just south, I suppose. You'll be wanting to go after him right away, then?"

"Yes, but I thought maybe we could spend the night here. We're awfully tired and so are our horses, and it's raining rather hard."

"Certainly, certainly. I'll see that you're awakened early, in time to make a good start."

Just then a servant poked in his head. "My Lady, are those persons staying?"

"Yes, Clive, just for the night."

"I'll tend to their horses, then, but I'll not deal with that dog!"

"Oh, Rus," Heather said. "Yes, send him in here to me. He's rather leery of strangers."

"He's not the only one what's leery, Miss. You can have him."

Dinner that night was a strained affair. Lady Brecon chattered nervously, and occasionally Heather pretended to listen. Welly concentrated on eating. The food was excellent, but the atmosphere was so tense that it hurt his digestion. Lord Brecon scowled silently throughout the meal and excused himself before it was over. Only Rus seemed to enjoy himself, sprawling over the hearth, each head chewing a meaty bone.

When the servants had cleared the table, Lady Brecon said, "Now, I'm sure you're both tired. Heather, you can have your old room, and Wellington may take the little one next to it. I'll have you awakened early."

Heather stood up. "All right, Mother. Thank you for putting us up." Briefly she glanced at her mother's tense face. There was something to read there, but it certainly wasn't love.

"Good night, then." Hurrying out of the room, she was followed by Welly and then Rus, a bone in each mouth.

Lord Brecon returned to the room after they had left. He held a green glass bottle in his hand. "Perhaps a little bedtime wine for our guests?"

"No! They didn't say anything about wanting those two. Morgan did give me some trinket for Heather if I should see her. I'll give her that, but I won't have her harmed."

Lord Brecon snorted disdainfully and left.

When Heather had shown Welly his room, she went into her own and sat on the bed, dejectedly twisting her braids. She wished they hadn't come here. They'd had to, of course, following Earl, but she had also hoped in the back of her mind that maybe it would feel like "home." It didn't.

She had moved to this house after the death of her father, when her mother married Lord Brecon. But it had been clear from the start that this plain, awkward child of a Scottish refugee father was an embarrassment to the household, and she'd been sent off to Llandoylan as soon as possible. Sighing, she looked around at the cold stone walls. She'd actually spent little time among them, and they certainly exuded no feeling of homecoming now.

She began undressing, angrily tossing her clothes on an old, ornate chair. Her mother seemed anxious to have her out of here. Well, she was no less anxious. Get some sleep and go. The less time she wasted in this cold dump, the better.

A knock on the door startled her. "Yes?"

"It's your mother, Heather. May I come in?"

Mechanically, Heather walked to the door and opened it. The woman stepped in looking around distractedly. Then moving the wet clothes to the bed, she gingerly sat down on the chair. "I . . . I'd like to talk a moment."

Heather felt herself tensing up, inside and out. Resignedly she sat on the bed.

Her mother smiled awkwardly. "I'm sorry we haven't been quite as close as we might have been, Heather. There are things we really don't know about each other, aren't there?"

Heather said nothing.

"I mean, for example, over the years I've discovered I have certain . . . talents. I picked up little skills, you know. And since I understand such things are often hereditary, I was just wondering if you'd found you had any?"

Heather frowned at her. "Magic, you mean?"

"Yes, I suppose you might call it that."

The girl was silent a moment. "Yes, I guess I do have a little power."

"Good. Well you see, I have something for you, then. It's an amulet. An old heirloom really. It sort of helps with those things. I don't use it much. Lord Brecon doesn't approve, you know. And I'd like you to have it."

She reached into a pouch and held out a lump of black stone, trailing a fine gold chain. When Heather looked at it closely, she could see it was not shapeless but roughly carved like the head of some beast. Two shallow depressions formed its eyes.

"Take it, dear. It's old and I'm sure quite valuable, as well as useful. I do want you to have it. After all, I've never given you much, have I?"

Heather reached out and took the amulet into her hand. It felt cold and smooth.

"Here, let me help you." Her mother quickly slipped the chain over Heather's head, disentangling it from her braids.

"Yes, it's right for you, I can see that. Well, I'd better let you get some sleep." She moved quickly to the door. "Good night, Heather."

"Good night, Mother."

Heather stood staring at the closed door. Her mother had some powers, too? And she'd given her a gift, an old family thing. Maybe she should have tried to know her better. Unexpectedly, she felt a trickle of regret.

She fingered the worn amulet. It was pretty enough in an odd sort of way. And it did feel as though it had . . . something to it. But she was too tired to experiment now.

She moved to the window to check that it was fastened against the rain—and almost screamed. A horrible yellow face was plastered against the glass panes. Bald, with a scraggly yellow beard, it had close-set eyes and two enormous ears. And it was saying something through the glass.

Curiosity vied with horror, and she moved closer. She could just make out the whiny words.

"Nice Lady. Glad you come. Help Great Wizard. Me show."

"Wizard! You know where Earl is? He needs help?"

"Plenty help. You bring other friend, too?"

"Other friend? Oh. Oh, I know you! You're the troll from the bridge."

"Yes, Nice Lady. But Troll not good at sticking to walls. Let in, maybe?"

Hurriedly Heather opened the other half of the window, and the troll scuttled in like a hairy yellow spider, rain dripping from its bedraggled fur. Rus jumped up and smelled him with both noses, then wagged his tails approvingly.

"Where is Earl? What happened? Oh wait, let me get Welly."

She rushed to the next room where Welly was already asleep. Soon he was standing beside her, staring with sleepy amazement at the troll.

"The little fellow from the bridge. I can't believe it!"

"Me not little fellow. Me fierce troll warrior, companion to Great Wizard!"

"Last I remember," Welly said skeptically, "that great wizard threw you off a bridge."

"Oh, that's water under bridge now. Hee, hee!" For a moment the troll curled up, laughing at his own pun. Then he straightened proudly. "But we good friends now. Great Wizard needs help."

"Where is he?" Heather asked anxiously.

"Downstairs. Way down in old cold dungeon. Troll look in window. Wizard not move for days."

"Oh, no!"

"He alive, or why they chain him?"

"Good thinking," Welly said. "But who are 'they'?"

"Lord and Lady here. Bad people. Trolls never nasty to guests."

Heather was already throwing on her clothes, a look of grim determination on her face. "Maybe not. But some people can be."

Minutes later the two were fully dressed with sword belts around their waists, and with the troll, were moving down a darkened flight of stairs. Rus, having been admonished to keep quiet, slunk along behind like a nightmare shadow. In a room below, they could hear Lord and Lady Brecon talking. Heather wanted to listen, to catch them in their treachery, but she knew she had to hurry on.

She had led the party through several passages when a servant suddenly stepped from a doorway. They threw themselves back around a corner. After a breathless moment, Heather peered out then scurried across an open space to a small wooden door, hurrying down the narrow stairway beyond. Shadowlike, the others followed.

Smoky, widely spaced torches lit the stairs and the dank passage beyond. Jumping anxiously about, the troll pointed to the end of the corridor. "Great Wizard there. They not lock door."

But when they cautiously peered into the far room, they could see no sign of the wizard.

Summoned to the manor door, Lord and Lady Brecon had hurried out of the cell, leaving Merlin gripped by despair as well as paralysis. In minutes, he thought, Glamorganshire soldiers would throw him over a horse and haul him like a sack down to Cardiff for that poisonous little Nigel to gloat over.

Still, it did seem as though his hostess had given him slightly the wrong dose. His mind was fully alert even if his body remained like stone. Perhaps if he tried focusing his mind. . . .

He slipped into relaxed coolness. Like rivulets of water, his thoughts ran through his body, feeling out the poison and flowing around it. It was everywhere, stretching its barbs into every fiber of his body. He tried gripping his thoughts around it, seeking to pry it loose. But the poison tendrils were too thin and widespread. There was little to get hold of. He struggled on and on until his mind, too, was exhausted and numb. Weakly he floated back to the surface.

The room around him was still empty, and his body was still motionless. Yet there was a certain tingling about his face and hands. Maybe he had pulled something loose. But it would never be enough, not to work an escape before the troops came, even if that hadn't been them arriving.

No, without some control of his body he could not work the proper spells. Yet his mind. . . . There were certain personal magics that didn't use the body, or even speech, that worked instinctively without deliberate action. He'd learned that several years ago before regaining the memory of who he was. Maybe if he couldn't escape, he could appear to have escaped.

He sank back into his mind. Unfettered by paralysis, his thoughts raced over his body, changing the way it reflected light. Lying motionless on the pallet, he slowly faded from sight until nothing but the dented straw was visible and the empty-seeming manacles.

Now if they came, they'd think he was gone. But suppose they searched, suppose they touched the pallet? They'd feel him there even if they couldn't see him. There must be some other clue he could lay.

The small, high window was dark now with night. And it was still latched shut. But if they were to find it open, they might think he'd escaped that way and search no further.

He concentrated on the vague tingling around his face. If he could just get out one word. His thoughts battled with the heaviness of his lips and tongue. He tore at it, shred by shred, like clinging vines. Slowly, slowly it began to drag away. Inside his mouth, his tongue twitched. Painfully his lips tingled, feeling less and less like stone.

He tried to form the word, tried again and again. Slowly he came nearer. There was a noise in the corridor. It must be now!

Like a spear, his thoughts shot across the room, dragging with them a word. Poorly formed and faint, still it was spoken. The window unlatched and blew open, letting in a cold, wet gust of wind.

Outside in the corridor, several pairs of eyes peered through the half-open door. "Great Wizard gone!" squealed the troll. "Not understand."

"Hush!" Welly whispered. "Someone's coming. Quick, in here."

The four ducked into an unused cell, tearing aside sticky sheets of cobwebs. A guard shuffled around a bend in the corridor. He muttered as he passed. "Why I got to check a prisoner what's chained to the wall and out cold . . . ?"

He shoved the door fully open and stomped into the cell.

"Wha . . . ? Chains still fastened, and look at that window! Great gods, he *is* a wizard!" The man rushed from the room, yelling for help as he pelted up the passage.

Welly, Heather, and the troll looked at each other in the gloom of their cell. They were about to step out when more voices and footsteps were heard.

"How could he be gone?" Lady Brecon demanded shrilly. "That drug shouldn't have worn off for days."

"If you've bungled this, my dear, and we've no one to send to Nigel. . . ."

They burst into the end cell. "Gone, all right!" Lord Brecon roared. "Slipped free of the chains and out the window. That's what comes of fooling with magic."

"It wasn't my idea to . . ."

"Shut up, woman! We've got to call out the guard and find him. Hurry!"

The footsteps rushed back up the corridor, while behind them four figures slipped from the neighboring cell and into Merlin's. They looked about the empty room.

"Well, at least he got away," Welly said, polishing his glasses on a dirty sleeve. "Now we've got to do the same."

There was a faint noise behind them like a whispering mouse. They turned and stared as the empty pallet and manacles slowly appeared to hold someone.

"Earl!" Heather rushed to the inert form.

"Can't move," he whispered faintly.

"Great Wizard fooled them!" the troll chortled.

"Yeah," Welly said, "but he's got to get out of here for real, before they check back."

"Earl, can you melt those manacles or something?" Heather asked.

He tried to shake his head but failed. "No," he mouthed.

"What'll we do?" Heather said, examining the solid-looking wall rings to which the chains were fastened.

"Heather, use your magic," Welly urged. "They may be back soon."

"But I can't deal with iron. All I'm good for is animals."

"Right," Merlin whispered.

"What? Animals? But how . . . ?" Slowly Heather turned to look at the only animal in the room. Rus's forepaws rested on the straw pallet as he whimpered mournfully.

Heather grabbed the furry paws in one hand. With the other she reached out for Merlin's cold, lifeless hands, bringing them together with a clatter of chains. Then she fell silent, her eyes closed, her body tense and rigid. She wasn't at all sure she could do this, but she had to try.

Very slowly at first, there came a change. The furriness she felt in one hand was gradually matched in the other. At last, the changing forces stopped passing through her. Drained, she opened her eyes, then laughed with delight.

The hands in the manacles were no longer hands but sleek furry dog paws small enough to easily slip free of the iron. Merlin's lips twitched in a smile.

"Heather, you're terrific!" Welly exclaimed. "Troll, check the window."

Toes and fingers finding every chink in the stone, the troll swarmed up the wall and peered out. "No people," he announced.

"Good. Heather, go get that chair from the other cell."

She slid Merlin's paws free of the manacles, then hurried out of the cell. Returning in seconds with a rickety chair, she placed it under the open window. Welly was already staggering to his feet with Merlin slung over his shoulder.

"Good thing he's so scrawny."

Welly climbed carefully onto the chair and passed his limp burden up to the troll. Once the wizard was dragged through the window, Heather handed Welly her squirming dog. Next came her turn, and finally with Troll and Heather each grabbing an arm, they hauled up Welly. He jammed firmly in the window. His legs flailed the air, and he groaned piteously as the others renewed tugging. Suddenly he popped through, tumbling them all onto the rain-wet grass. Scrambling to their feet and supporting Merlin between them, they moved quickly through the dark to a clump of low bushes. The earth smelled of mold, and the branches around them drooped with cold raindrops.

"We're outside the courtyard here," Heather whispered. "But we can't get very far with Earl like this."

"Me get horses," Troll said, and scurrying out of the bushes, he slipped through the open gate of the courtyard. Running about and shouting, the men with torches failed to notice one more shadow.

Then one guard searching the walls of the manor squatted down by the window they had just crawled through. "He came out here, all right. See how the grass is all trampled down?"

"Idiot, we know that!" another called. "What we want to know is where the skinny brat *is*, not where he was."

"Maybe *you* do," the other muttered. "If he's a wizard what can melt through chains, *you* go find where he is."

Still squabbling, the two returned to the courtyard and soon joined a mounted search party that clattered off down the road. A few minutes later, three dark horse shapes slipped out through the gate with the troll prancing in front of them.

"Troll good with horses, like Nice Lady. But not know how to do dog-paw trick."

"Oh, the paws!" Heather gasped. "I'd better try to change them back."

Merlin grunted agreement.

Welly looked at his friend and chuckled. "Good old Puppypaws the Wizard."

Heather clutched the hairy paws in her hands and closed her eyes. Frowning, she tried to remember how they ought to look. Why didn't she notice these things? Long thin hands, she thought, very, very pale, with bones and faint blue veins showing through. For good measure, she tried visualizing dog paws as they should be on the end of long, furry dog legs.

She opened her eyes and squeaked with alarm. Merlin's paws remained the same, and his arms were now distinctly furry.

Scowling, she tried again. Just concentrate on hands this time, she told herself. At last she felt, then saw, the familiar hands in hers. They even moved in a weak squeeze, which she gratefully returned.

"Can you stay on a horse?" Welly asked anxiously.

"I'll try," Merlin whispered.

They boosted him onto the black mare. He sagged forward over the neck, feebly twining his fingers into the mane. Heather laid a hand on the horse's neck urging it to go gently. Then she and Welly mounted up, and with Rus and Troll loping along beside, they trotted swiftly down the darkened road.

Behind them on the gate, someone saw and called out the alarm. But the dark was with them now. They had escaped.

twelve

Reunion in the Ruins

Using side roads and south-tending valleys, the escaping party eluded their pursuers. But with a proven wizard as the quarry, the pursuit was less than enthusiastic.

They rode through a cold, raw dawn and into morning, finally stopping at an abandoned farmstead. Moving more easily now, Merlin still felt appallingly tired. He gratefully slid off the horse and was content simply to sit in the weak sunshine against an old stone wall.

Welly happily noted that Troll had also brought their packs, which they'd not taken to their rooms, including, most importantly, the food. The wizard's staff and sword, which he'd left with his horse, had come as well.

While Welly doled out some food, Heather hesitantly explained to Merlin what had brought them after him. He didn't say much for fear that somehow a wrong word would send her back. His happiness at the moment felt too fragile even to question.

"Where to, now?" Welly asked finally, as he broke a large, greasy slab of cheese into five parts. Reconsidering, he split the dog's share into two, one for each head.

"Well, I am headed to Caerleon, and . . . I'd be most honored to have your company."

"Troll honored, too! Great Wizard needs many guards."

"It certainly looks that way." Merlin laughed.

As they shared the welcome meal, Welly said, "You came from around here, didn't you? Originally, I mean."

Merlin nodded and swallowed a bite of bread. "Southwest of here actually. I was born in Carmarthen." He glanced at Welly and chuckled. "Why are you looking so surprised? Even wizards are *born* you know, not hatched."

Welly blushed as his friend continued. "My mother was daughter of the local chief. But she wasn't married to my father. She wouldn't even tell most people who he was. He was Eldritch, you see, and that sort of thing was rather frowned upon. Rumors spread instead that my father was a demon, and needless to say, I didn't have the easiest of childhoods. Once I started learning how to use my powers, it was sore temptation to pay back my 'little playmates.' But I moved away, and sort of fell into the business of advising kings."

"Did you go back to Carmarthen often?" Heather asked.

"No, not often. But that was where I thought I was taking Nimue that last time." He was silent a moment. "We stopped on the way at a cave near Bedwas. They trapped me there. Nimue and Morgan."

Uncomfortable for his friend, Welly tried to sound matter-of-fact. "It was lucky those Gwent raiders spilled their salvaged dynamite where they did, or you might still be in that mountain."

"Lucky, perhaps, or fated. Like the age change. Was it just chance I was at the low end of that spell cycle I was using? If I'd been at the extreme old end, I wouldn't have been of much use to Arthur now. Though I've got to admit," he rubbed a hand ruefully over his smooth chin, "I wouldn't have minded a few more years of maturity."

Heather laughed, but Welly was still pondering fate. "But what about Morgan? You said we're bound to fight her. Is that fate, too?"

Merlin frowned and closed his eyes. "Morgan. She's part Eldritch, too, you know, but the power she cultivated is different from mine. It has other, darker sources. She used those to sustain her life, and she'll use them, if she can, to win control of this world. Arthur's goal of peace and unity never suited her, because the kind of power she wields works best in chaos and ignorance. She can dominate that kind of world.

"And she's making another try at that now. That's why I must find that bowl. It might give us some glimpse of her plans; it might give us a fighting chance."

Heather shook her head. "And Morgan's not the only enemy we have, it seems. Not with Nigel as King of Glamorganshire."

Merlin snorted. "Nigel's just a petty tool. Dangerous, yes, but not smart enough to be a major actor." He was about to add something about Morgan's role in the plot to poison him, but a glance at Heather's strained face silenced him. She'd clearly been feeling bad enough about her mother's betraying him to King Nigel. It would hurt her needlessly to learn that her mother had also been dealing directly with Morgan.

He changed the subject. "Welly, are you thinking of dropping by and seeing your folks at Aberdare?"

"I was, but we'd better skip that. Nigel knows that I'm from there, and he won't be any too happy when his bounty hunters report that you've gotten away."

Merlin laughed. "I hope never to be a position to make Nigel happy. Let's be on our way."

As they continued south, the weather varied between cold and dry, and cold and wet, with rain occasionally turning to sleet in the evenings. In three days' time they reached the outskirts of Caerleon.

Merlin shook his head in bewilderment as he looked at the sprawling town. The fifth-century settlement he had known had been a small, affluent Roman town, only slightly decayed after the withdrawal of the legions. Now, later centuries of buildings sprawled over the landscape, most abandoned and fallen into weedy ruin.

In gray mid-morning, the companions rode through the town gate. Troll, hidden under a blanket, rode behind Welly, steadily grumbling to himself. In front of an inn, a little girl was walking along a low wall, balancing herself with much flailing of arms. Merlin pulled his horse up beside her.

"Young lady, would you be so kind as to direct us to the really old part of town, some Roman ruins, maybe?"

The girl looked him and the others over, taking in their good horses and the swords at their belts. Then she jumped down and ran toward the inn. "Grandpa, there's a bunch of rich tourists here who want to see the old Roman stuff."

In seconds a bald old man bustled out, wiping his hands on a stained apron. He smiled as he saw the travelers. "Well, well, young people out to see Caerleon's claim to fame. Afraid there's not much left, but if you poke around some, your trip'll be worth it, I dare say. A big Roman city and fort there was. Golden domes, the books say. Very grand.

"Now the old baths, what's left of 'em, are right down there. Turn to your left where the road jogs. Then the theater, that's off to the right at the next crossroads. There's a field they say used to be barracks, just humps in the ground mostly now. But the theater's pretty impressive still."

"Thank you, sir," Merlin replied. "But what about houses, those golden domes you mentioned?"

"Well, I dare say they were all over once. But they've been built on since, you see. Why just last year we dug up some old tiles in our cellar. It's the same all around here, but not much to see unless you're a mole." He laughed heartily.

Merlin nudged his heels into his horse. "Well, thank you, innkeeper, we'll just keep to things above ground."

"And after your sightseeing, young sirs and madam, you won't find a better beer or finer victuals than we serve here."

"Thank you. We'll keep that in mind."

As they trotted on, Welly said, "This bowl of yours, would anyone have left it in a bath?"

"I shouldn't think so. Those were big public baths. Let's start with the theater. Arthur used to hold court there when the weather was good. I ought to be able to get my bearings and figure out where the houses and villas were."

The theater proved to be a large oval depression. Brittle weeds filled the center arena and climbed over the stone mounds that once had been seating.

"How do you expect to find an old bowl in a place like this?" Welly said when they'd dismounted and walked into the amphitheater.

Merlin sighed. "I've no vision of where it is, none at all. But I'm sure that if I'm close, I'll feel it. I put so much of myself into it, there must still be some link."

Slowly he began walking around the remains of the theater and the area nearby. The troll trotted along eagerly, occasionally stopping to dig in places of his own, exclaiming over whatever bits of rubbish he unearthed. Rus happily helped the troll dig, while Welly drifted off to explore the barrack remains. Heather was left alone in the theater.

After looking halfheartedly about, she sat on a grassy mound and thoughtfully twisted a braid. Was there any way she could use her powers to help find Earl's bowl? Probably not. Her magic seemed totally linked with animals. And unless a mouse was curled up in the bowl, she'd probably never see it.

But what about the amulet? She had tried to forget that. After what had happened at Brecon, she wasn't sure she wanted anything of her mother's. Still, if the amulet was a family heirloom, it was rightfully hers now. And maybe it did have some powers, ones she could use that weren't tied to animals. She touched the chain at her throat and slowly pulled the amulet from under her shirt. It was worth a try, anyway.

Heather studied the black stone. What sort of face was carved there? It could be either human or animal. In its sunken eyes, high cheekbones, and pointed chin, she saw no expression at all, only a sense of cool power.

She stood up. The stone felt smooth and cold in her hands. All right. She'd look for silver. Closing her eyes, she filed her mind with thoughts of silver, bright and smooth, gleaming like unclouded moonlight.

As she walked slowly around the amphitheater, the amulet tingled in her hands. She walked on, and it burned like cold fire. Suddenly excited, she dropped to her knees, scrabbling in the dirt. Her fingers tore through grass and damp soil, then touched something small and hard.

Eagerly she pulled it out and scraped off the dirt. A small disk, and it was silver! She rubbed and spat on it but couldn't quite make out the inscription. A coin showing some ancient queen. It wasn't Earl's bowl, but it was silver.

This was exciting! She tried again, and before long she had recovered another coin, a badly tarnished thimble and a silver ring. The ring was far too big for her. She could give it to Earl. But no. Somehow she didn't want to tell him about the amulet. He was probably just as bitter as she toward her mother. And anyway, this was her magic. She'd work with it on her own for a while, then maybe she'd tell him once she could handle it better.

She dumped her treasures beside a rock where Troll found them almost as soon as he returned to the theater. He jammed the ring on his thumb, and jumped about proudly showing it off. But Merlin when he rejoined the others was too discouraged to show much interest.

"Well, it certainly isn't around here." He sighed and sat wearily on a pile of stones. "Of course, it may not be anywhere near Caerleon now, but I'd better check the rest of the town. There was a big villa Arthur used as his residence when he stayed here. I should be able to find that site. And there're several other possible spots as well."

Welly groaned. "Can we eat first, maybe at that inn?"

"Yes, why don't you all rest and get something to eat. It'll be quicker if I do this on my own. But better stay away from the inn. We are in Glamorganshire, after all, and the less public notice we draw, the better."

"Troll go, too. Great Wizard need guard. May find more poison wine."

Merlin laughed, holding a hand to his head. "No fear. I think I've sworn off wine for the rest of my life. But come along, you're a first-class digger."

The wizard set off with his staff and troll companion. It was beginning to rain in earnest now, and taking some food from a pack, Welly and Heather crowded into the ruins of a little building beside the theater. Staring out into gray sheets of rain, they ate in silence, sharing tidbits alternately with Rus's right and left heads.

After a time the rain let up, turning at last to fine mist. Bored with doing nothing, Heather walked again into the center of the theater, and Welly followed.

"What sort of theater do you suppose this was?" she asked looking around the enclosure. "The kind they fed people to lions in?"

"Maybe," Welly guessed. "But I bet they did real plays, too. Those ancient Romans and Greeks had a bunch of famous playwrights."

Heather struck a theatrical pose. " 'Friends, Romans, countrymen, lend me your ears'!"

"That's Shakespeare."

"I know, but that's the only old playwright I've read. 'To be or not to be, that is the question'!"

"Bravo," a sharp voice said behind them. "But there is no question about you being my prisoners."

The two spun around. A rank of horsemen was standing in the misty rain beyond the rubble walls. Foremost among them was Nigel Williams, King of Glamorganshire.

"Nigel!"

"What a pleasure to meet old schoolmates again," he said dryly.

"Eh, yes," Welly said, recovering. "A lot's happened since Llandoylan, hasn't it?"

"Yes it has, Frog Eyes, and I still remember our parting. Actually I'm quite pleased to find you both. When I rode up to Brecon, I had hoped to lay my hands on only your pallid friend, a present for a certain ally of mine. Of course, I do have my scores to settle with him as well, but I'll have to leave that to her. You two, however, are all mine."

With a gesture from Nigel several of his warriors dismounted and stalked toward Welly and Heather. The two drew their short Eldritch swords.

"Oh, ho!" Nigel snorted. "The little vermin have sprouted stings. Careful, boys, I want them alive, for now."

In the low hills above Caerleon, Merlin stood on a bare knoll, kicking dejectedly at featureless stones.

"It's no use, Troll," he said, more to himself than his companion. "I thought maybe here, where they had a little summerhouse. . . . Arthur and Guenevere came here sometimes. There were always some bits of treasure about."

He stamped his staff angrily onto the ground, ignoring the scorched hole it left. "Oh, Troll, it was so lovely here! At sunset in summer the air was soft and warm, and there were birds in the sky and flowers in the grass, rich green grass. It's such a loss, such a horrible senseless loss!"

"Your bowl?"

"No! No, this world—or what it was. How could people have become so filled with hate that they were willing to destroy that beautiful world?"

The troll frowned, furrows rippling over his bald head. "Me only know this world. Not even seen much of Faerie. But Mama's seen lots; say it pretty place. Like this place once, maybe?"

Merlin smiled. "Yes, they were very much alike. But maybe it's better to know only one world. Then you don't break your heart comparing."

"Troll's heart not broke. But stomach empty. Go back to Nice Lady and Brave Warrior?"

"And full saddlebags? Yes, let's."

They had almost reached the theater again when the troll, who had been eagerly scampering ahead, came slinking back, eyes wide as saucers.

"Trouble, Great Wizard. Bad men with horses catch friends. Tie up like rabbits."

Cautious now, Merlin hurried forward. Nearing the theater, he crawled onto an old wall where he could look down into the stone-circled depression. Welly and Heather, tied hand and foot, lay on the wet grass. Beside them, the dog was totally swathed in ropes with particular attention to its muzzles. Merlin could tell from the sword slashes and bites several of the soldiers nursed, that the capture had not been easy.

There were few soldiers to be seen now, but he could sense others out of sight, probably waiting to ambush him. He slid quietly off the wall, whispering for the troll to stay back.

Down in the theater, Nigel sat on a stone, cleaning his fingernails with a dagger. "Pity you wouldn't tell me where your washed-out friend's gone," he said to his bound and gagged prisoners. "It would have saved this tiresome wait. But I expect he'll be back soon. You three dears seem so inseparable. Morgan tells me you've all taken service with that Northern upstart who calls himself King Arthur. Sounds like the sort of mangy charlatan you would take up with. Though, frankly, what you three misfits could offer anyone, I don't know."

He got up and sauntered over to the bound dog, kicking it roughly in the ribs. "Except maybe this warhound of yours. He has possibilities, he's mean enough."

Strolling back to the wall, he casually threw his dagger into the turf. "But to be equally frank, I can't understand what the lovely Morgan wants with that scrawny troublemaker. She gave me some song and dance about his being a dangerous wizard. Ha! The day Earl Bedwas is a dangerous wizard is the day I grow donkey ears!"

"Better get some new hats designed, then, Nigel."

The young king spun around. His former schoolmate was standing inside the theater.

"How did you get. . . ? Well, never mind." He motioned down the soldiers who were scrambling to their feet. "I'll take care of you myself. I suppose you've acquired a pretty little sword like these children here?"

"I have, yes. And a few other weapons. But I think we should talk, Nigel. You, after all, are King of Glamorganshire now. And I am advisor to the King of Cumbria."

"Yeah, yeah, I know. King Arthur Pendragon riding out of legend! Just your sort of madman."

Merlin struggled to keep his voice calm. "Regardless of your opinion of his historical claims, he does hold the kingship of Cumbria and alliances with Carlisle, Newcastle, Cheshire, and the Scots. You may find yourself dealing with him someday. And in any case, your current alliance with Morgan is most ill-advised."

"For you, yes, since I'll be turning you over to her; but she is just the sort of powerful friend Glamorganshire needs."

"Powerful, yes. But Morgan is nobody's friend but her own. I'm simply warning you Nigel. Beware of her."

"My, how I appreciate your concern." He looked around to see the rest of his troops moving back into the theater. "But now that we've had our friendly little school reunion, it's time to get on with business. Take him, men!"

The soldiers charged forward. Swiftly Merlin brought up his staff, pointing it at his three captive friends. Their bonds suddenly writhed with life and slid off. Like snakes, the freed ropes twisted in the air, stretched out, and multiplied, until a swarm of wriggling ropes swept toward the astonished soldiers.

They raised their swords against them, but for every rope they hacked, two slithered down their sword arms and twisted around their bodies. The soldiers and their king yelled and struggled, but within moments they all lay on the damp grass like flies enwebbed by a spider.

Lowering his staff, Merlin walked over to the feebly struggling bodies. He looked down at Nigel, who glared at him through the web of ropes. "The day Earl Bedwas is a dangerous wizard, is the day you grow donkey ears? Whatever you say, Nigel."

He flicked his hand towards the bound king's head, and two long hairy ears sprouted up between the entwining ropes.

Welly and Heather were now on their feet, helping each

other off with their gags. Heather looked at Nigel and could barely keep from laughing. "Earl, I've had enough of Caerleon. Can we leave now? People look a little odd around here."

"I think that's a splendid idea. Welly, why don't you get our horses. I've a few details left here."

As Welly headed in one direction, the sounds of neighing and thumping hooves came from another.

"Reinforcements?" Heather said in alarm.

Looking through openings in the stony banks, they saw the soldiers' horses in panicky flight away from the town. The troll bounded in through one of the gates.

"Great Wizard tie up bad men. So Troll tell horses go away."

"Good work," Welly said, leading their own mounts.

As they mounted up, Merlin held up his staff again. "We don't want the neighbors setting this lot free too soon."

He swept the staff through the air around the perimeter of the theater. On four opposing banks, mist curled up, purple-red mist. It spread and thickened and began to take form—the form of four good-sized griffins. They stretched, then folded their wings along their lean lion bodies. With beaks open and tongues flicking, they fixed glowing eyes on the suddenly quiet captives.

"Let's go, kids," Merlin said turning his horse toward one of the theater entrances. "Glamorganshire's a lovely place to visit, but I believe we've outstayed our welcome."

He paused, then looked back at Nigel, who couldn't speak for the rope running between his clenched teeth. The king's donkey ears twitched angrily.

"Regardless of what you may think of us, Your Majesty, I strongly advise that you stay clear of Morgan. Alliances with her are very one-sided."

He kicked his horse into a trot, and the three humans and one troll left the ruined theater. Rus gave his former captors a parting chorus of growls then followed after the others, his tails wagging jauntily.

thirteen

Pursuit

They rode swiftly out of Caerleon, then stopped to consult the old maps Welly had brought.

"Those ropes were real enough, but the griffins are just illusion," Merlin said as he examined the tracery of pre-Devastation roads. "A nice touch, I thought, but they'll fade. Somehow, though, I don't think we need worry about being followed."

"Speaking of nice touches," Heather said, "I did like those donkey ears."

"Oh, they'll last only a month or so, but I probably shouldn't have done that. Arthur's wise old adviser deliberately humiliating the king of another shire. But Nigel's such an ass!"

Welly laughed. "Well, you can't deny he asked for it."

After a steady ride eastward, they came at last to what once had been the estuary of the River Severn. Under a great steel bridge, it had fanned out and emptied into the

Bristol Channel. But now the ocean had receded, its waters locked up in northern ice, and the bridge spanned an empty valley, dry except for the now narrow Severn, doggedly cutting its way through the ancient silt.

As they followed the old road, the bridge towered above them. Five hundred years of neglect had left it rusty and twisted. The soaring cables, which had once linked the twin towers, coiled down like dead snakes, and the shattered roadway sagged toward the water.

The troll, however, was enthralled. "Ooh, look at bridge! Look at bridge!" he chanted in ecstasy. "Troll dream of bridge like that!"

"You'd have to be a mighty large troll to defend that bridge," Merlin pointed out. "Besides, I don't think the tolls would be very good. Looks as if it's not used much."

He headed his horse along a dirt track that cut through the old estuary to cross the diminished river on a makeshift bridge of stone and scrap metal. The troll rushed ahead and, sticking his head over the side of the bridge, shouted out several fierce-sounding phrases. Then he trotted cockily back to the others.

"Safe to cross now. Troll lead famous wizard and warriors. Nobody bother."

After they'd crossed, Heather rode up beside Merlin. "Doesn't he have some name besides 'Troll'?" she asked. "I mean, what would we call him if he were among a bunch of other trolls?"

"Oh, he must have a personal name. But folk of Faerie are awfully private about such things. There's a great deal of power tied up in their names. I suggest that if we ever find ourselves among a bunch of trolls, we give him a name of our own."

Welly had ridden up beside them. "Maybe something like Clancy or Wilberforce or . . ."

Heather wrinkled her nose. "I think 'Troll' is just fine."

Having crossed into the relative safety of Gloucester, they camped for the night and started south again early the next day. As Heather rode along, the amulet kept swinging into her thoughts. She could feel it, a cold exciting weight against her chest. She wished she'd thought to use it when they were attacked at Caerleon. But she really didn't have any idea of how to work it. It seemed to be some kind of focuser, a conduit of power that freed her from having to go through animals. The idea made her oddly uneasy but excited as well. The countryside about them was drab and uninteresting, and each of her companions seemed wrapped in his own thoughts. She'd experiment.

Letting her horse fall slightly behind the others, she slipped the amulet from under her shirt. She thought about a focuser, focusing power the way a lens focuses light. All right. Thinking about flames, she gazed beyond the black shape in her hand to the dry, brittle-looking bushes along the roadside. For minutes of monotonous riding, she kept at it until suddenly she saw a wisp of smoke rise from one of the bushes. She turned in her saddle as they passed and saw the twigs burst into pale flame.

An excited thrill of achievement—and guilt. Quickly she looked ahead, but no one had seen her. She was unsure why she felt a need to keep this secret. But the cold stone clutched in her hand gave her a heady feeling of control and independence. And somehow its secrecy was part of that.

She practiced with the amulet through the day. Each time her tie to the thing seemed to strengthen so that working it became easier. The day's ride now seemed a good deal more interesting.

But while Heather's mood improved as the day progressed, Merlin seemed to become more and more uneasy. Occasionally he stopped his horse and looked about, or stood in the saddle, head tilted as if listening to something just out of hearing. Finally, Welly asked what the trouble was.

"I'm not sure. I've just a vague sense of being watched, of being followed, maybe. It's very indirect, as if the observer's either far away or cloaking itself somehow."

Uneasily Welly scanned the gray landscape. "What do you think it is?"

"Well, there's no doubt that there are folk from Faerie

about. They could be watching us out of curiosity. But somehow, I don't think it's quite that innocent."

"Oh?"

"There's a faint whiff of Morgan about this."

Heather shivered as if hit by a cold wind. "You think she's after us?"

Welly said, "Nigel could have sent her a message that we'd escaped."

"He probably did. And I'm sure she wants me as a prisoner just on general principles. But for now, as long as she doesn't know what we're after, I don't think she'll interfere. She seems to be keeping some sort of tabs on us though. Can't say I like it."

The three rode closer together. Picking up their uneasiness, the normally far-ranging dog and troll closed ranks as well.

At the small town of Cheddar, Merlin turned them from the main road. "This route heads our way," he explained, "and it used to be one of the loveliest in Britain. I almost hate to see what's happened to it, but surely the cliffs are undamaged."

The ancient crumbling road narrowed as it climbed, sheer cliffs rising on either side. Before long, buttresses of stone towered above them. Looking upward, they could see jagged rocks tearing against gray sky. Mostly the rocks were bare, the elemental bones of the earth exposed in a deep raw wound. But here and there dampness trickled out of a cliff face and ivy cascaded down in a shower of dark wind-ruffled green.

Welly and Heather found the place stark and slightly daunting, but Merlin was enthralled. "Look, there's still some ivy, even some ferns. I'm willing to bet they don't survive here just by chance. Troll, would you say there are any folk of Faerie hereabouts?"

"Oh yes, Great Wizard. Think so. This strong place. Me see." Before they could say a word, he had leaped off into the rocks and bracken.

"Shouldn't we wait for him?" Heather said as they rode on.

Merlin looked around. "He'll catch up. Beautiful as it is here, I don't think we want to linger. There's something . . . something wrong."

The silence in the rocky gorge weighed down upon them as much as the glowering cliffs. Muffled clumping of horse hooves echoed and reechoed between the rock walls, but that was the only sound save the trickle of an occasional spring as it seeped out of the rock like blood through wounded skin.

With a sudden rustling and clattering, Troll appeared before them. "Great Wizard right. Plenty rock sprites here. But they not talk much. They afraid."

"Afraid of us?" Welly said, surprised.

"No, no. Happy see Great Wizard and friends. Afraid of something else. Something coming."

Whatever it was, the horses seemed to sense it, too, and quickened their pace on their own.

Heather slid a hand under her shirt and felt the amulet. Perhaps this would tell her something. It tingled under her touch. The longer she held it, the colder it became, yet she could learn nothing from it. Maybe she should ask Earl how to use it. The thought filled her with reluctance. This was nothing she wanted to share just yet. Perhaps if she . . .

A screech sawed through the air. Fearfully they looked up. A winged black shape darted through the narrow band of sky above them. It cried again, then banked sharply and headed back, joined by another. More like flying snakes than birds, they shot along the gorge. Then, with wrenching screams, they dove toward the riders.

The horses neighed in terror. Merlin's bolted off in one direction and Welly's in another. Heather's mount reared so suddenly that she was flung from its back. Lying half stunned on the earth, she grabbed at her amulet, trying to work it against the flying things. It did nothing. One creature veered and dove directly at her. She scuttled to the shelter of a boulder just as the screaming shadow whipped by her.

Regaining some control over his horse, Merlin was working back toward Heather, filling the air with bursts of fire.

But in the narrow confines of the gorge, these kept missing the dodging targets.

There was a sudden silence as the attacks ceased. Holding his staff high, Merlin looked anxiously about to see why. Silently one of the creatures dropped from its perch on the clifftop. Wings outstretched and jaws open, it hurtled like a spear toward the wizard. But as it moved down, a tendril of ivy uncoiled from the cliff and ensnared the creature in midair. Wings entangled, it jerked sharply, snapping the vine loose and plunging out of control to the rocks below. Sprawling beside Merlin's shivering horse, the thing twitched once then lay still. From above came a single mournful cry, and the second creature shot away like a black arrow.

Heather did not want to crawl from her shelter and look at the thing. Closing her eyes, she concentrated on her horse and on Welly's. In a short time, both animals plodded up the road, with Welly limping behind.

When Rus found her and began licking her face with both tongues, Heather finally abandoned her hiding place and joined Welly and Merlin by the dead creature. It was black and long, a scaly snake body with wings, and it stank as if it had been dead for days.

The troll slipped from rocks at the base of the cliff. Merlin looked up. "I believe we have your friends, the rock sprites, to thank for snaring this thing."

Troll nodded, smiling broadly. "They happy to. Say snakes belong in rocks, not sky. These bad."

"Well, they smell bad, too," Welly said, covering his nose. "Let's get going."

"Right, but just a minute." Merlin got off his horse and walking to the base of the cliff, piled several stones into a rough pyramid. Then he yanked three black hairs from his head and placed them on the top stone. Kneeling, he muttered a few words, then got up and returned to the others.

"What was all that about?" Welly asked.

"A thanks offering," his friend replied. "A token of friendship and trust. The folk of Faerie generally don't take part in the battles of men, but when enemies of their own are involved, they can be very useful allies. That thing does stink. Let's go."

They passed out of the gorge without further incident, though somehow the cliffs seemed less hostile and lifeless than before.

The following day they sighted what might be flying snakes several times, distant black specks against a pale sky. That evening, fire streaked like poison darts across the crimson sunset.

Camping in flat open land, the travelers felt uncomfortably exposed. Merlin conjured a large fire, and they huddled around it eating their meal and flicking occasional glances up into the darkness.

Finally Welly, Heather, and Troll wrapped themselves in blankets and curled up on the ground to sleep. Rus snuggled in beside Heather and was soon snoring with both muzzles. Wrapped in his own blanket, Merlin leaned against a rock by the fire and kept first watch.

Heather could not fall asleep. She closed her eyes, but visions of flying snakes darted vividly through her mind. The occasional real shrieking of one in the high distance sent shivers through her. Shifting restlessly, she rolled over and watched the firelight play over Merlin's gaunt features. He seemed lost in thought. She sat up.

"Earl, where are we headed next? Camelot?"

He looked toward her, his eyes slowly blinking back into focus. Sighing, he rubbed a hand over his face. "I had planned that, yes. In the daylight you could see the hill south of here. But now . . . I think we'll try somewhere else first."

"Why? Didn't you say that's where the bowl would have been taken if it weren't at Caerleon?"

"True, but it might not have stayed there. Once Arthur was gone and his kingdom falling apart, the royal treasure would probably have been moved somewhere safer. Glastonbury, I should think."

"Glastonbury? Where's that?" Swathed in her blanket, she shuffled closer to him and the fire.

"West of here. It was a village, a small one, but it had

a church and monastery, probably the oldest in Britain. The monks there were good friends with us at Camelot, particularly a Brother Joseph. He was a young fellow and used to come over to gossip and play chess." For a moment, the wizard seemed lost in a dreamy distance. Then he focused on Heather again.

"Arthur's told me that after that final battle—it was fought right around here by the River Cam—the wounded, himself included, were taken to Glastonbury."

"Is that where . . . ?"

"Yes. It was from there that he was taken off to Avalon. A hill there, Glastonbury Tor, was a main entrance to Faerie."

He was silent a while until Heather asked, "And you're certain *all* of the king's treasure would have been taken to those monks?"

Merlin shook his head. "No, I'm not but . . . but frankly, Heather, I don't want to go to Camelot if I can avoid it. It will be a bare weedy hilltop, and I'll remember it with wooden palisades, banners snapping in the wind, laughing people, faces I knew. I would . . . rather not deal with that now."

His voice cracked. Hesitantly Heather placed a hand on his, but could find nothing comforting to say. Finally he continued. "That's my problem, you see. I'm too tied to the old world, to its memories and ways of magic. Even now I'm circling through the old sites, searching for an old tool that might not even work in this world."

The desolation is his voice was unbearable. Heather struggled to change the subject. "Earl, there's something I've been wondering about. I know how you survived all those years enchanted in that mountain. And you've said that Morgan probably survived by having some unscrupulous dealings with death. But she wasn't locked up in a mountain. What did she do all that time?"

"Morgan?" He smiled bitterly. "Oh, make trouble, I imagine. Of course, her powers would have weakened as the strength of magic did. But come to think of it, I suspect she was quite comfortable in some of those later centuries."

"How so?"

"Well, her magic was always very cold, very 'thing' oriented. And from what I've read, those last pre-Devastation years were quite thing-oriented as well. They must have been, I suppose, for people to allow their *things* to destroy them."

The two sat for a while in silence, cold pressing on them from one side, the fire's heat from the other. Heather looked at her friend. "And that's what you're trying to stop from happening again, isn't it?"

"Yes, that and whatever Morgan is planning for our immediate future." Angrily he crushed a twig he'd been toying with. "But the question is: *How* do I stop it, any of it? If that bowl doesn't work, what then? That's the only sort of magic I know. Sometimes, despite all our 'power,' I suspect that both Morgan and I are irrelevant in this world. We have our little magic toys and play our little magic games. And they work, in their way. But still we don't fit—not in this new world with its new magic."

"But Earl, remember talking about how all this might be fated? If there is some overall pattern, then. . . ."

A nerve-tearing screech sliced down at them. Heather dove to the ground as Merlin hurled a hasty fireball into the air. The creature's gaping mouth glowed red as the flames flew past. It veered away. Shooting upwards, it joined a half-dozen others circling overhead.

"What was that?" Welly said, sitting up and groggily groping for his glasses.

"One of Morgan's little toys," Merlin replied.

"Ooh, me saw!" Troll said jumping about excitedly. "Great Wizard singe nasty snake's wings. Next time shoot one down in flames."

"Next time?" Heather questioned, huddling closer to the fire.

Merlin sighed, looking up at the black forms circling in the darkness above. "I can see that this is not going to be a particularly restful night."

fourteen

Treasure Long Kept

When dawn finally came, the snakes broke formation and drifted eastward, finally disappearing into the orange smear of sunrise.

"What a night," Welly groaned as he unwound himself from his blanket. "How many of the little beasts did you incinerate?"

Wearily Merlin started to answer, but Troll piped up. "Three, me count!"

Merlin nodded, yawning. "Yes, though I think the last one was just singed. But I don't believe that Morgan sent them to seriously threaten, just to harass. Right now, I think she's more curious than dangerous."

"Well, I feel plenty harassed," Welly said. "I can put up with a lot of abuse, but a good night's sleep is sacred."

Merlin laughed. "Once we get going today, everyone had

better keep an eye on each other so no one falls asleep and gets left in a heap by the roadside."

The road that day proved to be a long and dreary one. The land was featureless with distant hills, dark against a gray sky. A few stone farm buildings huddled beside fields of muted green crops.

Once more, Heather's thoughts were dragged to her amulet. Last night when the flying snakes were attacking, she'd felt a nagging urge to grab and use it. But part of her kept warning that she didn't know how, that it had worked badly in the gorge, and that anyway Earl could handle things. It was her comfort in Earl's presence that finally shut out the nagging. In the end, she'd tried to lie so that the cold black stone couldn't touch her skin. She was reluctant to take it off all together, but when she couldn't feel its tingling cold, she was more at ease.

Now however, anything seemed better than the boredom of the trip, and she tried experimenting with it again. Rippling the grass as from an unseen wind, or making rocks roll along the road behind them was great fun. But after what Earl had said last night, even this play made her a little uneasy. If this was some magic tool from the old, old days, maybe it really ought not to be used now. And besides, anything her mother had used. . . . No, that was probably unfair. Still, the power didn't feel quite right for her.

The sky lowered as the day wore on. Clouds tumbled over one another, turning darker and darker shades of gray. Against them, the shape of Glastonbury Tor grew steadily larger. Occasionally they saw black things slipping between the clouds. And at times they caught glimpses of movement among rocks and ditches as they passed.

"Earl," Welly said uneasily, "that hill you mentioned, is it still an entrance to Avalon?"

"No, not to Avalon. That is the home of the Eldritch, and they've closed most of their doors to this world. But there are many parts of Faerie, all very different, though some share doors. What do you say, Troll?"

"What, Great Wizard?" The creature bounded up on its spindly legs.

"Those little shadowy things we've been seeing, are they out of Faerie?"

The troll sidled closer to Merlin's horse and looked around nervously. "Yes, from Faerie, but not from Troll's part. Other parts—dark things there."

"And are they coming through the Tor?"

"Me think so, yes."

Merlin frowned. "Which means we're heading into a hornet's nest. If Morgan wants to cause us trouble, she's got ready-made helpers. And whatever happens, she mustn't get that bowl. That would give her far, far too much power." He thought for a moment, then looked down again at their small yellow companion. "Troll, is there any chance that the Tor also opens onto your part of Faerie?"

"Don't know. Maybe." Suddenly he sprang up excitedly. "Oh! Great Wizard wants Troll to go on secret mission. Fetch help. Be hero!"

"Well, if we have to face an assortment of Faerie's darker folk, it might be useful to know if there are any willing to rally to the other side."

"Yes, yes. Troll go. Fetch help. Big hero!" Quickly he jumped over a roadside ditch and disappeared into the gray landscape.

"Do you think he'll bring help?" Heather asked.

"Hard to say. Most folk from his part of Faerie aren't strongly committed one way or another. But they're not averse to fighting if the mood strikes them. Like those rock sprites at the gorge. Actually, this area was once full of swamp sprites, and they made powerful friends if you could interest them."

"Swamp sprites?" Welly looked around. "It's dry as a bone around here."

"Yes, now. But it used to be all swamp and lakes. Glastonbury on its hill was almost an island, with a little dock down near the base of the Tor. People must have drained it later for farmland."

As they approached the town, their road climbed out of the lowlands. It passed ruined outskirts and entered finally through recently refortified city walls.

The arrival of three mounted warriors and their extraordinary dog caused quite a stir. Market booths clustering around the old stone cross were beginning to shut down, but there were still plenty of people about to point and ask questions.

One stout, authoritative-looking man walked up to Merlin. "You young people on your way to join the king?"

"That depends on which king you mean."

"Why Edwin of Wessex, of course. He's called for all able-bodied fighters to rally to him at Uffington. I'd go myself if I were a bit younger, that I would."

"I'm certain you would. But, you see, my companions and I have recently ridden here from Wales and are rather out of touch with events in these parts. What is the threat that causes your good king to head for Uffington?"

"Indeed, you must've been under a stone of late! Take no offense, none was meant. It's the armies of the East under that witch woman of theirs. Rumor has it they are ready to move on Wessex."

"Rumors!" said a second man. "We've had rumors of those easterners for months and not seen a one."

A short gray-haired woman bustled up. "Oh? What about the muties attacking flocks down near Salisbury? Those aren't rumors, and they say the witch controls them too."

The first man nodded his head. "And if it's rumors, then King Edwin takes them mighty seriously, because I've heard he's called on those two in the north, the Scottish queen and King Arthur himself."

"More rumors! And if you believe that King Arthur story, you're more of a doddering old fool than I thought!"

"Huh, that shows how much you know, Jedediah!" the woman said. "That King Arthur is as real as these three youngsters here. Why, he's united half the shires in the North already."

"Maybe so. But you can't pretend he's the *real* King Arthur."

"Who else but the real one could have done a thing like that, I'd like to know. Besides, they say he's brought back his old wizard, too, and they work magic—a lot bigger magic than Sam the tailor or the old henwife do."

"Bah! You're not going to catch me believing in a fairy-tale king and a crazy graybeard wizard. I've got sense!"

"Jedediah, if that old wizard were to hear you say a thing like that, he'd turn you into a centipede. What do you say, young people? You've been traveling."

All three suddenly developed a cough. But finally the eldest recovered and said, "Ah, yes, I suppose he might. Though maybe into something less nasty, a goose perhaps. But friends, you say Arthur is to join your king at Uffington?"

"That's what they say," the stout man replied. "Will you be going there, then?"

"Yes, I think we might. But first we have some business here. Could you tell me where the church is?"

"Which church is it you want? There's Saint Mary's and Saint Michael's, the New Zoroastrians, the Armageddonites, the. . . ."

"I mean the old church, the very old one."

"You mean the abbey? That's supposed to be the oldest church in England. It's nothing but ruins now, has been since way back."

"No matter. That's the one we want. Where is it?"

"Just down the road and beyond those walls. But if it's praying before battle you're looking for, there's no clergy there."

"Thank you, but we're looking for something else."

As they rode down the street, Welly and Heather were still quivering with laughter. Merlin shot them a squelching look, then chuckled.

"Maybe once I finally start growing a beard, I'll dye it gray, just to live up to expectations."

The dark afternoon was slipping into a darker dusk. Yet as they passed through the enclosing walls, there was still enough light to see the ruins of the once-vast abbey. The building was a great shattered shell. Roofless now, it was paved only with weeds. Remaining segments of wall soared upward, holding empty windows against the sky. Here and there among the ruins, crouched rare hawthorn trees. In the dusk, their blossoms shone a ghostly white.

Merlin shook his head. "This place certainly grew after I saw it last. Then it was just a couple of wattle-and-daub buildings with a fenced-in churchyard. Now the trick's going to be finding just where that old church was."

He dismounted and, clutching his staff, wandered toward the east end of the sprawling ruins. There the roofless span was widest. Suddenly uneasy in the growing dark, Welly and Heather hurried to join him.

As Merlin walked slowly about, concentrating on stones and weedy soil, the attention of the other two kept shifting to the darkness beyond the walls. Shadows seemed to flit there, just out of sight. Whimpering, Rus crowded up to them, both tails stuck between his legs.

"Earl," Welly whispered, slowly pulling out his sword. "I don't think we're alone here." But the wizard, poking at some stones with the end of his staff, didn't seem to hear. Shrugging, Heather unsheathed her own sword. The two followed their friend, keeping eyes on what they couldn't quite see.

Deliberately they criss-crossed the open space, then passed through an arch in a lone fragment of tower. Suddenly something snapped out of the darkness. Wrapping a scaly paw around Heather's ankle, it yanked her to the ground. She slashed at it. Her sword met something solid, and the air was sprayed with rank liquid. Shaking, she scrambled to her feet to find Welly struggling with some dark, entwining shape.

Spinning around as if suddenly awakened, Merlin slammed his staff on the ground. Purple flame shot from its top, illuminating the scene. The creature wrapping itself around Welly shrank back, but not before they clearly saw its many hairy arms and bulbous head.

Heather nearly gagged at what the light showed of her own attacker. Her sword had slit open its scaly hide, and entrails now lay steaming on the bloody grass. Turning away she took several shaky breaths and walked to where the wizard was now kneeling beside a dip in the ground.

"Please, Earl, let's come back and look in the morning. This place is . . . occupied at night."

Standing, he headed off in a new direction. "I don't think it is normally. They're here because we are. All the more reason I must find that bowl now. Morgan's getting much too interested in us."

"But suppose it isn't here either?" Welly said anxiously.

"I . . . I think it is. Somewhere." He continued walking westward, questing like a hound following a scent. As he walked, his staff shed a heatless pool of light about him.

The others stayed near but kept turning around as they walked. Where the light faded into darkness it reflected back from eyes. Some were low to the ground, some high up. A sudden shriek and something dove at them from the sky. Annoyed, Merlin raised his staff, searing the underside of wings. It veered off screaming.

Fearfully lowering her gaze, Heather saw eyes again. Their numbers had grown. "Earl, could we hurry? We're attracting a lot of attention."

"Yes, yes," he said absently. "Keep them back, I've got to concentrate. We're closer now, I know it."

"Well, keep your light going!" Welly begged as the flame on the staff faded. It flared up again, but emboldened by numbers, the things in the dark were closing in.

Something all teeth and claws darted toward them. Welly swung at it with his sword. It dodged back, but another scrambled in from behind. Heather spun around, nicking it with her blade.

Suddenly, cries and the sound of fighting erupted around them. But who was fighting whom? Even Merlin noticed the change, and his staff shot out a new flare of light, showing a battle raging on all sides.

Constant motion confused the picture, but clearly none of the combatants were human. Among them jumped a yellowish creature, jabbing and thrusting with a great pike.

"Troll!" Heather cried. "He's brought reinforcements!"

Desperately now, Merlin continued his search as the strange battle surged around them. Suddenly the noise of fighting shrank under a new sound, a flapping of giant wings. Cowering, Heather and Welly stared into the dark sky.

Great black wings hovered overhead, then lowered slowly to one of the central towers. Now, above the third tier of arches, something crouched like a living gargoyle.

"Merlin!" a clear voice called from above. "Stop poking about in the dirt. I wish to talk with you."

High in the wall, an empty stone niche glowed with green. In its center stood a pale woman, black hair flowing about her shoulders. A hideous creature sat hunched on the wall above her.

Angrily, Merlin looked up. "Perhaps, Morgan, but I don't wish to talk with you." He moved quickly to where an arch led to a smaller more intact section of the ancient building.

"Such a rude child!" The woman laughed coldly. "I've been keeping an eye on you, you know, ever since you slipped away from that incompetent Nigel. You are obviously looking for something, Merlin dear, and I've decided the time has come to see what it is."

Motioning the others to follow, Merlin hurried down some weed-choked steps beyond the arch. "If I am looking for something, it is nothing of yours. So you can just take your misbegotten pets back to wherever you crawled from."

"But, Merlin, your interest is recommendation enough. Whatever it is, I intend to make it mine!"

She thrust forward her hand, and a spear of green light shot toward them. Merlin flung up his staff, deflecting the assault. "Troll!" he yelled. "Get your people in here. Now!"

On the fringes of light, the scuffling forms shifted and creatures scuttled toward them. Merlin jerked up his staff and shot a glob of purple flame toward the figure on the wall. It smashed against the glowing green stone, shattering into a shower of sparks.

"Poor aim!" came the taunting reply. "But I don't want to play games, little boy. I want what you are looking for."

By now, an assortment of creatures had slid down the

stairs to join them. Some were thin, wispy things and others were as chunky as stone. One looked something like Troll, only much larger.

Merlin leaped again to the top of the steps and shouted something, staff raised high above his head. Snakes of purple flame jumped from the staff to the sides of the arch, then rapidly crawled upwards. Spreading along the tops of the walls, the flames encircled the western end of the ruins. Every empty window and broken wall glimmered with purple light.

Beyond the barrier of light, Morgan screamed and hurled a mass of green flame. It shattered harmlessly against the purple wall. Enraged, she rained down volley after volley, but the barrier held.

"That had better hold long enough," Merlin muttered as he turned away. "Now, I must find it!"

The air crackled with light and choked them with the stench of ozone and sulphur. Half-blinded by the glare, Merlin suddenly stepped into nothing. Crying out, he plunged into the ancient crypt, gashing his forehead on a stone at the bottom. Blood ran down his face as he dizzily pulled himself to his knees.

Still stunned, he stared down into the growing pool of his own blood. Something was there, moving beyond the surface. A figure running through the darkness, running through a fenced churchyard. A guttering torch showed the worried face. Brother Joseph. The now elderly monk hurried on. Saxon raiders attacking the town. He must hide the church treasures, especially those that had been Arthur's. The Saxons must not desecrate them!

The robed figure came to an alcove of stones and hurried down the worn steps. At the bottom lay a stone slab and a crude wooden cover. He yanked the cover aside and from his bulging robes pulled out clattering handfuls of things. They glinted briefly in the torchlight before dropping into the darkness of the well.

The pool of water shimmered and changed into blood. Whose blood? Merlin passed a hand over his eyes. Had

Brother Joseph survived the attack? But that was over, long over. And at last the secret had been passed.

The wizard staggered to his feet. The barrage was still heavy about them, but the purple glow seemed fainter.

Heather was calling from above. "Earl! Earl are you all right?"

"Yes," he croaked.

"The barrier's weakening!"

Already he was running to the left. "Yes. I'll be back soon!"

He found what he sought, an opening in the crypt wall and steps leading down. By the light flickering along his staff, he saw a carved stone arch at the bottom. It was later work, but below it was the same stone slab. The hole in it, glinting slightly from damp, was choked with trash and stones. Dropping to his knees, he frantically pulled at the rubble with both hands. Some was jammed firm. He could hear shouts and fighting again from above.

Desperately he rammed the point of his staff into the stones, letting power flow down the shaft, he pried the fill away. Then dropping the staff, he reached into the cold water, down to the mud beneath. His fingers groped about, touching various objects. But they sought only one and tingled with kinship when they found it. Scrabbling at the smooth, round shape, he pulled it free of silt and water.

In trembling hands he held it. Its intricate designs were obscured by mud and tarnish. But he knew it, and it him. They remembered so much.

The shouting from above called him back. Rubbing at the blood still trickling into his eyes, he scrambled up the stairs and emerged into the night. The purple light had faded to a flicker, and all about him creatures were fighting.

Morgan took no part now, content to watch her minions win from her perch on the broken wall. But when she saw Merlin again, she shouted her triumph. Holding both hands above her head, she drew power about her into a pulsing green mass. More potent than anything she had launched before, she hurled it now toward her ancient enemy.

Merlin recoiled. His staff was below, out of reach. Instinctively he raised a hand to shield his face. The bolt of power slammed downward, striking the bowl. With a deafening blow, it rebounded back. Sorceress and gargoyle screamed as the reflected power sheared off the top of the tower, leaving smoke and silence behind.

Groggily Merlin sank to his knees, looking at the now gleaming bowl in his hands. "Well, that's one way to clean old silver," he muttered before slumping unconscious to the ground.

fifteen

The Hill of the White Horse

The pre-dawn light was gray and cold. Merlin stared up into it, wondering chiefly about the pain in his head. Slowly he raised a hand to find bandages wrapped around a throbbing forehead. As he struggled to sit up, the jacket that had been thrown over him slid from his shoulders.

"Well, welcome back," Heather said limping toward him. The whole left side of her body was burned, the boot on that side nothing but a few sooty shreds.

Others hurried toward him. Welly's right shoulder was wrapped in a bloody rag. Rus was missing half of one tail, and a ragged gash running across Troll's forehead ended in a severed ear. Looking absurdly unbalanced, he grinned from ear to former ear.

"Great Wizard find bowl and blow away nasty witch. Troll proud."

Merlin found his voice. "We'd never have lasted long enough without your recruits, Troll. Where have they gone?"

"Oh. Some hurt, some killed. They go back. No like to stay around humans. Some muties they not mind. But plain humans scare them."

"They don't like us," Heather said, "yet they fought and died for us?"

"They not like humans, but like to fight! And like witch and friends even less. Besides"—the troll proudly straightened his squat body—"folk of Faerie very learned. Know Great Wizard. Happy to help."

"Well, I was happy to have their help."

After they had breakfasted, Merlin tied the bowl to his belt by one of the three metal rings at the rim. Welly looked at it, then frowned slightly.

"Earl, we haven't found any trace of Morgan. Did that blast completely incinerate her?"

"I doubt it. That bolt did carry most of the power she could muster, but it probably weakened in the reflection. I imagine she's off somewhere nursing hurt body and pride.

"And speaking of hurt bodies, let me try a little healing magic, at least for the burns and cuts. I can't do much for missing tails and ears, I'm afraid."

Soon Heather's burns and the gashes Troll and Welly sported were reduced to tender redness. The painful cut on his own forehead became an angry scar, which he tried vainly to hide behind his ragged black hair.

When they finally rode away from the abbey ruins, they found fearful, curious faces staring from windows and doors. The events of the previous night could hardly have been missed, and the group's appearance now was particularly impressive due to the presence of the troll.

Merlin recognized several citizens from the conversation of yesterday. "I'm afraid, sir," he said to the stout, authoritative gentlemen, "that we have ruined your ruins a little further. But King Arthur and your own king will be grateful."

"Ah"—the man nodded knowingly—"so you do have something to do with Arthur. All the rumors are true, then? The real Arthur has returned?"

"Indeed. As has his graybeard wizard. But tell your doubting friend I won't turn him into a goose after all." He ignored the open-mouthed stares and furtive hand signs. "Now, if you want to help defend this fine town of yours, I suggest you send all able-bodied fighters to Uffington. The kings and queen may well need them."

Their ride eastward from Glastonbury took several days. On the way they encountered parties of Wessex warriors rallying to their king's call. They also noticed occasional shadowy forms flitting along the roadside, but they felt none of the uneasiness such sights had brought earlier.

"Troll, are these friends of yours?" Merlin asked one night as they were setting up camp in a ruined farmstead.

"Don't know most. Faerie is big place."

Welly unfastened the saddle girth under his horse's shaggy belly. "But I thought you said your people didn't care much about wars between humans."

"They don't," the troll agreed, looking hopefully at the food bags Heather was unloading. "But this not just human war. Something big coming. That witch calls up folk from dark parts, folk we not like."

Merlin was squatting down arranging rocks for a fire circle. "What Troll means, I believe, is that if Morgan's forces have netherworld allies, so do we. Not as many perhaps, nor as visible. But they're coming from all over, I can feel them."

Heather felt them, too, an occasional mist blowing across field or streambed, or dream shadows flitting by while they slept. But she didn't probe at the feelings. And despite its nagging, she firmly ignored the amulet. It had burned at her during the fight, but she hadn't taken the time to try using it. Now she felt she'd seen enough of high magic, and to stifle the stone's stirrings she took it off and stuffed it in her pack. She was content to be with Earl and the others and to touch at the thoughts of passing animals.

Merlin was enormously relieved to have the ancient bowl swinging at his side again, but he hesitated to put its old powers to the test. Better to wait until they were back with Arthur, and he could concentrate on it. In the meantime there would be several days' riding with his friends.

Friends. He was surprised at how happy that term made him. Heather and Welly and even Troll were here not simply because they wanted to help in what he was doing, but because they wanted to help *him*, to be with *him*. The idea was so new it frightened him, though he dared hope that somehow in this new world it might last. Sometimes as they rode along, he and Heather exchanged smiles. He wondered what she was thinking and feeling but couldn't bring himself to harden things into words.

The villages they passed while riding eastward were alive with rumor. It was said that a great army had arrived from the north led by Arthur Pendragon and the flame-haired Queen of Scots. They had joined with King Edwin of Wessex at the ancient hillfort above Uffington. From everywhere, would-be warriors, both men and women, were streaming to join them.

The eagerness of these people to fight and face death awakened Merlin's uneasiness. He saw again the startled face of John Wesley, bloodily clutching the king's banner. How many other such faces would haunt them in the end?

His somber thoughts lifted slightly when the chalk downs came into view. For miles they formed a bold southern wall along the Vale of the White Horse.

As they rode up the shoulder of the downs, Heather looked eagerly about her. A fresh, cool wind rolled in pale waves over the grass and blew wisps of hair about her face. "Did they have a lot of white horses here once?" she asked.

"Maybe," Merlin replied, "but the name comes from one horse in particular. It was so old people had forgotten its origin even in my time. I wonder if, after all these years, it could still be there?"

"A horse?"

"Yes." Then his voice quickened with excitement. "Yes, look! Look at that hillside."

Heather squinted ahead. "I don't see anything, just some scars in the grass."

"But they form a pattern. Don't you see it?"

She stared again. "Well, maybe. Oh yes. Yes, I see it. A prancing white horse!"

"Thousands of years ago, people cut that figure through the turf down to the white chalk. And ever since others have kept it from growing over. I imagine no one knows why anymore, just keeping faith with the past."

Welly's gaze slipped to the slopes above the stylized animal. "Is that the old fort up there where those people are?"

Merlin's sigh was tinged with regret. "Yes, we're almost there."

As they rode up the steep hillside, what had appeared to be a natural plateau resolved itself into a large enclosure surrounded by a ditch and two massive banks. The ancient fortress's command over the sweeping countryside was dramatic. Only to the east did the shoulder of the downs obscure the view, and there a rock and turf watchtower was already being built.

As they rode through the camp, only a few heads turned. Many recruits were new since Chester. But then a tall young man with a golden beard came running their way, and attention swiveled onto them.

"Merlin, you old truant, you're back! You wouldn't believe how I've missed you, prophecies or not." The king smiled at the others. "I knew your friends would bring you back safe." Then his gaze stopped at the troll. "And you have a new friend, I see."

Merlin nodded toward his one-eared companion. "Troll here is my loyal bodyguard. And," he lowered his voice, "you may have noticed a few more recruits of his general sort in the shadows."

Arthur nodded. "They seem to be gathering in the hills beyond the Ridgeway. Most of our troops are keeping well clear of there, trying not to see anything. But I, for one, welcome the help."

"For one? Merlin questioned. "And how are you and the fiery Queen of Scots getting on these days?" Merlin had seen the lady in question striding toward them, red hair tied back with a golden band.

Arthur turned and addressed her. "My lady, this old wizard asks how you and I are getting on at present."

She smiled as she walked up to them. "About as well as two captive fell dogs, always at each other's throat and lost without each other's company."

She deftly ducked Arthur's mock cuff, and Merlin smiled. He didn't need a bowl of prophecy to see how things were developing there.

In the days that followed, they settled into camp life with the army growing around them. Merlin finally turned his attenion to the bowl. He spent hours sitting by himself at the edge of camp, the bowl filled with water and swinging on a tripod before him.

He saw visions, but they were confused, oddly removed and displaced, as though glimpsed through a distant window. The more he tried to look at them squarely, the more they slid away, fleeting visions at the edge of sight.

What he did see was distorted and strange, twisting currents of time coiling through past and future toward a blinding blast of white hate. It had to do with Morgan, he knew, and with battle, but the only message he could extract was a vague compulsion, a need for movement to the southeast.

Day after day he spent by the bowl, trying to drag the vision closer, to shake it into focus. He scarcely ate or slept, and when Heather brought him meals, she often found the last one untouched.

Sometimes Heather would simply sit with the wizard, though he seldom pulled himself away from the elusive vision to note her presence. She was surprised at how content she was simply to be near him, to sit on the turf bank watching the wind silver the grass or watching the cloud shadows chase each other across the land below.

One afternoon as she left in an effort to find Merlin some tempting food, Kyle came up to her. They hadn't spoken a great deal since her return. He had been busy with his music and the attentions of young ladies of the camp. But now he stepped deliberately in her path.

"Heather, I don't like to meddle. But you're too good a

person to sink into some dark, useless sort of life. Why don't you leave the wizard to his brooding and join the rest of us?"

Her frown deepened. "Kyle, a while back you were telling me I had to choose. Well, I suppose, I have chosen. I know where I belong or at least with whom I belong. Now please let me be!"

She stomped away, anger smoldering. But in one thing she knew Kyle was right. She might be less torn by indecision now, but she *was* rather useless. Welly, when not with the cook's assistant, was spending his time training new recruits. Even Troll was busy with the growing troops out of Faerie. Earl, she felt, did need her, but she really wasn't being of much use to him.

Wandering dejectedly back to her campsite, she decided there was still one way she could help him. Reaching into her pack, she pulled out the amulet. Despite an occasional itch to use it, she hadn't put it on since Glastonbury. Slipping the chain around her neck, she knelt down on her blanket. She might not understand or fully trust its powers, but she had to try something. If only she could figure out how to channel it.

But it was difficult. The power of the amulet was of a cold and alien sort, nothing like the animal-tied magic that came so easily to her. Clearly it was closer to Earl's high magic so if she could just use it, surely she could be of some help to him.

Suddenly like a bolt of lightning, fear blasted through her. She wanted to help Earl, and he was indeed in terrible danger. Bathed in sweat, she gazed at the shiny black surface of the amulet. It sank away like a dark tunnel. She fell through it, and pictures rushed past her. Massive rocks in a sunlit circle, their patterns ancient and meaningful. Mounded earth over the cold and decay of a stone tomb. The pictures were clear and precise and reeked of threat. Threat that only she could save him from.

Welly, walking by to fetch his sharpening stone, noticed Heather crouched on her bedroll, shaking as if in a fever.

"Heather?" He walked over and knelt beside her. "Heather, what is it? Are you all right?"

He noticed the amulet and her frozen gaze. Covering its riveting blackness with a plump hand, he shook her shoulder. "Heather, come out of it!"

She fell back with a cry. Looking wildly at him, she slowly realized who he was. "Oh Welly, I've got to help him!"

"Help who? And what is this?" He raised his hand from the black stone.

"It's a magic amulet." She no longer felt a need to hide it, not from Welly. "My mother gave it to me, it's an old family piece. It showed me . . . Welly, Earl's in terrible danger, and I have to go right away and save him from it!"

"Earl is sitting by the north wall brooding over that bowl of his. He's not in any danger."

"Not now, but soon. If I leave now and go where I've seen, I can still save him from it."

"Why don't you just go to Earl now and tell him about it?"

"No!" She closed her fist possessively around the amulet. "Then he'd want to see and go there, too, and that would be the greatest danger."

"I don't see that."

"But I do. I *see* it. And I'm going right now." She stood up and fastened her sword to her belt.

"You can't go alone."

"I'll have Rus."

"Don't be crazy, that's not enough!" He looked after as she strode off to the horse corral, her dog padding behind her. "Aren't you even going to tell someone or leave a note?"

"No time."

Furiously he pulled off his glasses and started to polish them on his shirt. Jamming them back on his face, he ran to catch up with her.

"You coming, too?" she asked matter-of-factly.

"I have to. Earl would turn me into a swamp rat if anything happened to you. But this whole thing is crazy, and you know it."

She smiled grimly and picked out a tall, fast horse for herself.

A few minutes later, Heather and Welly, with Rus at their side, rode out of the south gate and along the ancient trackway that ran over the crest of the downs. Shortly afterwards a gray shape slid from the ditch that encircled the fort and glided from shadow to concealing shadow until it reached the campsite of Merlin the wizard. From folds of misty clothing, it pulled a scrap of folded parchment and pinned it to the bedroll. Then, like a puff of acrid smoke, it slipped away.

Hunched by his bowl near the north wall, Merlin sighed and sagged back with fatigue. Again, visions had danced and jibbered at him just out of reach, leaving him with only a sense of dread and a vague compulsion for the southeast. Shuddering, he looked up to see Arthur standing over him.

"Merlin, I've been standing here talking to you for five minutes. You've been somewhere else entirely, and by the look of you, somewhere you're better off away from."

Merlin sighed wearily. "Yes, but somehow I've got to make this work. There's danger out there, terrible danger, and maybe a solution. Morgan has some dreadful plan, I can feel it. But this Bowl of Prophecy is the only way I know to see it."

"Maybe, old friend, but don't kill yourself in the process."

The king squatted down beside him. "And I'll tell you something else, less mystic perhaps, but also important. We need water. Those two springs on the hillside aren't enough any longer for this horde. When the old Celts used this place as a fort, they must have had a well. Can you find it for us?"

He stood up, pulling Merlin shakily to his feet. "Come on. Put your wizardry to some down-to-earth use and find us some water."

His friend laughed ruefully. "You're right. Maybe I should give up on prophecy and concentrate on removing warts and divining water. Then at least I'd be of some use."

He looked about, really seeing the fort for the first time

in days. It bustled with soldiers and horses, and the turf ramparts were steadily rising. He turned his thoughts to wells. "I'd better use my staff; wood has an affinity for water."

"I'll send someone for it. You still look a little tottery. Heather says you haven't been eating enough." The king waved a beckoning arm at Kyle, who was walking by talking with a Scottish piper.

"Kyle, would you trot over to Merlin's campsite and bring us his staff? Don't look so alarmed; it won't turn into a snake. Will it, Merlin?"

"Not if I don't ask it to."

Despite this assurance, Kyle could think of a good many errands he'd rather be sent on. Near the king's tent, he found the spot where the wizard had stashed his things. Among rolled-up blankets, a saddlebag, and several cooking pots, lay the slender staff. It's wood was pale and smooth except where it knotted into a clawlike root at the top.

Gingerly Kyle reached for it, then saw the note pinned to the bedroll. On the outside, "Earl" was written in Heather's distinctive round script. Kyle picked up the staff, which felt reassuringly woodlike, then unpinned the note, deciding he'd take that to the wizard as well.

He returned to where Merlin and Arthur had been joined by several of the king's engineers. Merlin took the staff with a nod of thanks, while one engineer was saying, "It really ought to be within the banks, but we haven't found any stones or depressions."

Merlin stood still, closed his eyes a moment, then slowly began walking toward the southwest. The others, followed at a distance.

Kyle stayed behind, watching. He hadn't had a chance to give Merlin the note. Well, he would when they'd found the water. But now he wished he'd taken no part in this sending of notes between the two. He had to admit that the wizard was a good enough fellow, but his kind shouldn't get mixed up with regular people. And despite Heather's few tricks, Kyle felt she belonged in the normal world.

He wondered what message she had sent. Making some

assignation, perhaps? Or asking about some mystic formula? Maybe Merlin was having her act as his agent with those outlandish things lurking about south of the fort.

Curiosity vied with courtesy. The note wasn't sealed. He'd take a quick look.

"Dear Earl," the note began. That very familiarity annoyed him. He read on. "I want you to know that I am leaving with Welly. The time has come for me to make a choice. Welly is of my world in a way you can never be. Your world is right for you, but it frightens me. I want a simple, normal life somewhere, and I am going off to find it. Please don't follow us. This way is better." Signed, "Heather."

Astonished, Kyle stared at the note, quickly rereading it. So that was the choice she'd meant! He hadn't given her enough credit. It was a shame though that she'd had to leave them all, and for that he blamed the wizard. But Kyle guessed that Merlin would pay for it. Cold fish that he was, he seemed genuinely fond of Heather—of Welly, too. He might take this pretty hard.

Kyle folded up the note and looked guiltily about. The wizard, king, and others were gathered around a spot near the southwest wall. The harper walked toward them.

"Dig here," Merlin was saying as Kyle approached. "There'll be stones two feet down where it was filled in. Another three feet, and you'll hit water."

The engineers looked doubtfully at one another. Merlin shook his head wearily. "It's there. Do you want me to do the digging, too?"

The others smiled sheepishly, but Arthur said, "In this army we specialize. Wizards find water, and engineers dig for it. Come on, Merlin, I want you to get something to eat before you go back to glowering at that bowl."

As they walked off, the king's arm over the wizard's thin shoulders, Kyle stepped up. "Merlin, I found this note pinned to your blankets when I went for the staff."

Merlin flushed slightly when he saw the handwriting. "I'll

be with you in a minute, Arthur. I want to tend to this first."

The king nodded and walked briskly away. Kyle had already left, almost wishing he'd torn the thing up. He didn't like to see people hurt, not even odd magical people.

Merlin opened the parchment and read it. He felt as if he had stopped breathing. Each word cut him like ice. He tried to read it again, but his eyes blurred. Slowly he folded the note, slipping it into his shirt. Inside him, cold spread into numbness. Quietly he headed for the north gate and walked out into the gathering night.

sixteen

Emptiness and Peril

Through that evening and into the night, Heather and Welly rode along the Ridgeway. When Welly wanted to stop, Heather urged them on, finally allowing a few brief hours of sleep before prodding them on again.

Welly knew how attached Heather was to Earl and could understand her worry over some mysterious danger to him. But there was something odd about her now. When they had left Chester, spurred by her vision of the hawk, she had been worried but otherwise her usual self. Now, after whatever she had seen with the amulet, she seemed obsessed. Saying nothing, she kept her eyes intently on the road. Needing no map, she drove them along roads and over the countryside as if on the end of an invisble line.

By mid-afternoon the horses were staggering with weariness, and Welly urged that they stop. It wasn't like Heather, of all people, to be so inconsiderate of animals. Rus was so tired, Welly carried him for a while across his saddle. Heather's only response was, "Not now, we're almost there."

They were off the downs now, heading through fields of dry grass. Sheep bleated their annoyance and scattered out of their way. After a distance, a road they had joined cut through a wall-like mound of earth. As they passed through, Heather sighed, letting her weary horse stumble to a halt.

"This is it. This is what I saw exactly."

Welly looked around. They seemed to have entered a huge earthen ring, a ditch running around the inside of the high bank. Where it rose up again to ground level, the circle was repeated by a ring of massive upright stones. In places the circle was incomplete, but one could see where it had once run.

"Look at the size of those stones," Welly marveled. Running off in both directions, the unworked boulders jutted out of the earth like gigantic decayed teeth. Even Welly could feel the awesomeness of the place. But the locals seemed undaunted. Not only were sheep grazing beside the stones, a small village nestled inside its circuit.

Heather looked around as well, but with an air of scientific detachment, as if trying to read a pattern in the stones.

"Ah, I think that's the way we want to go," she said pointing to the right.

"No it's not." Welly was looking straight ahead at a rambling thatched building signed THE RED LION. "What we really want is a break at that inn."

"Wellington Jones! Here Earl is in mortal danger, and all you can think about is eating and drinking!"

"That's not fair, Heather! I've gone with you all this way. The horses are exhausted. Even your crazy dog is tired out. It's nearly sunset. Why don't we stay here and head off to wherever else in the morning?"

"Because that may be too late. Come on, it's not far now."

"That's what you said before. Isn't this the place you saw?"

"I saw it, yes. But it's only the first part of the pattern.

There's an avenue of stones that leads from here. We follow
it to . . . to wherever it points."

"And where is that?"

"It's . . . a place. I don't know for sure. But I have to
see the pattern before the light fades, or I might miss it."

"Oh, all right, all right. I'm just along as a trusty sword
arm. But take it slowly, will you, for the horses at least?"

As they rode by the Red Lion, Welly gazed longingly at
the half-timbered building, looking cozy and welcoming under its thatch. Through a window he glimpsed a snug little
room with low beamed ceilings and a large fireplace. Then
he wrenched his eyes away toward the brooding stones, their
shadows stretching long and cold in the late afternoon sun.

Soon they rode out of the circle. Before them marched
an avenue of stones leading off to the southeast. Right again,
Welly thought. Uncanny. He preferred it when Heather talked
with horses and sheep, even fell dogs.

They followed the double row of stones over a rise and
down into a swale. There the markers disappeared.

"Well, where to now?" Welly asked grouchily.

"Just follow this bearing as if the stones continued. We'll
see it from the top of that rise."

Welly sighed wearily, but already Heather was urging her
tired horse upward.

A cold evening wind grated harshly against their faces.
At the top of the rise, Welly looked about. To their right
was an odd-looking conical hill. He figured that was peculiar
enough to be their goal, but when he glanced back to Heather,
she was looking straight ahead.

"There it is. You see that bump?"

"No."

"It's right on the horizon, a long, low hump."

He looked where she was pointing. Barely discernible
along a distant ridge was something resembling a raised scar.

"That?"

"Come on." Riding down into a valley they passed through
the tumbled ruins of a long-empty farmstead. After they had

forded a small stream, their way began rising again. When the long mound appeared on the ridge above them, Heather halted her horse.

"Let's walk from here."

Welly groaned. He was too tired to walk an inch. Then guiltily he patted his shaggy horse. The poor beast must feel the same, with far better reason. He slid from the saddle, fixed the reins to a stone post and trudged up the hill after Heather and Rus. Grass rustled in the cold breeze, and a lone bird called forlornly from the grayness overhead.

Ahead of them the western sky was stained red with sunset. Silhouetted against it, the long mound looked dark and ominous. As they drew closer, Welly could see several large stones looming up sharply at one end. The whole thing seemed extremely unwelcoming.

Once they'd reached the mound, it was clear that the stones marked some sort of entrance.

"Are we going in there?" Welly asked dubiously.

"Of course."

"What sort of place is it?"

"An old tomb, I think."

Welly shook his head. "No Heather, we really don't want to go in there."

"It doesn't matter whether we *want* to or not, we *have* to."

Rus, however, clearly shared Welly's doubts. Sticking his one and a half tails between his legs, he flopped down by the farthest stone and whimpered.

Ignoring him, Heather walked through a narrow gap in the stones into a small open courtyard. Then bending down to clear the lintel, she stepped into the dark of the tomb itself. Very reluctantly Welly followed.

Light filtered through ragged gaps where ceiling stones had fallen through, but it failed to penetrate the blackness of several chambers that branched off from the main passage. Welly was relieved when Heather passed these by.

The passage itself was narrow and low. Its stone walls felt cold as death, and the chill air smelled of earth and damp decay. The mass of rock and soil above seemed to weigh heavily down on them. Despite the bone-numbing cold, Welly felt sweat break out all over him. He wanted fervently to be elsewhere. Abruptly the passage ended, much sooner than the length of the mound had suggested.

The final chamber was small and round. On its earthen floor lay a large flat stone. A hole in the roof let in a thin mist of light. By it they saw a black lump lying on the stone.

"There's nothing in here," Welly said anxiously, feeling very much that there was something in there. "Let's go."

"No wait. What is this?" Heather knelt down and examined the black thing. She reached out her hand, but then drew it back. "Why it's a piece of charred wood."

Welly squinted at it in the fading light. It did look like a sooty piece of old root. "Yeah, probably part of someone's campfire. Please let's go."

"But I think this is important."

"It is, my dear," said a voice from the passage behind them.

Welly squeaked and leaped over the stone. Spinning around, he saw a woman standing in the passage, a woman with long black hair and green eyes. A ball of green fire glowed coldly in her hand.

"Morgan!" Heather gasped. She clutched at her amulet then snatched her hand away as the stone seared her palm with cold.

"Ah, you brought back my amulet. Good. I'll take it now."

"*Your* amulet? It is not! My mother gave it to me. It's a family heirloom."

"Oh, is that the story she told you? Resourceful woman— she has promise even if she did muddle the drug in the wine. No, my dear, I told your mother to give that to you in case you should come her way. I thought it might be useful."

"You . . . you mean . . ."

"I used it to keep tabs on you all. Every time you played with it, the ties strengthened. Finally they were strong enough for me to call you here."

"To call me? I came here because Earl was in danger!"

Morgan laughed. The chilling sound bounced back and forth in the tiny chamber. Heather and Welly huddled back against the cold, damp stones.

"And so he will be. But I need you out of the way first. Now, give me my amulet."

Reaching up, Heather snapped the chain and hurled the amulet against the fallen stone. It cracked sharply in two. "I should have known it was evil. Only animal power is right for me. I should have guessed."

Morgan stared at the broken amulet, her mouth compressed into a thin, hard line. "Breaking that means nothing, fool! It was an old thing, just a tool, and it's done its work nicely. Now, pick up that wood."

"No!" Heather glowered back at the sorceress.

"Don't put on airs with me, brat! I'm not playing at a battle of wills with some barnyard witch. Pick it up!"

Heather shrank back against Welly. Laughing contemptuously, Morgan hurled her green flame at the stump of wood. The flame smashed on the stone, rocketing the wood up toward the two cowering figures.

Heather thrust up an arm to ward it off, and the wood grazed her. Everything shattered apart. Her splintered mind screamed for help.

The world was loud and filled with terrible sensation. Blades of cold seemed to slice their bodies into strips, strips of being that stretched impossibly thin. The strips twisted and coiled, suddenly wadding together and hurtling into bottomless darkness.

When Merlin failed to join them that evening for supper, Arthur was annoyed. But when the wizard was nowhere to be seen the following morning, he became concerned.

After questioning several people, he learned that Merlin had been seen climbing down the hill of the White Horse early the evening before. The king was just considering whether or not to set out after him when his harper stepped hesitantly forward and told him about the note.

Arthur's face shadowed in remembered pain. Abruptly he turned from the harper and strode out the north gate. Scrambling down the steep hillside, splayed with its giant white horse, he stopped for a moment by the animal's single eye. Below he saw a lone figure, no, two figures, on distant Dragon Hill. The odd square hill rose abruptly from the fringes of the chalk, a last assertion of the downs before giving way to the wide vale below.

Arthur half ran, half slid to the bottom of the slope. Crossing an ancient road, he struck off toward the flat summit of the hill. Once there, dirty and out of breath, he saw Merlin seated on the ground staring vacantly across the valley. The troll huddled miserably nearby.

When he saw the king, the creature hopped up and scuttled to him. "Glad King is here. Great Wizard very sad. Not talk, not even eat."

Slowly Arthur walked over to his friend and sat beside him. The other never blinked.

"Merlin, it's me, Arthur. Please come back, please listen to me."

As though pulling his mind from some distant dragging sea, the wizard turned a blank expressionless face to the king.

"Merlin, I know about Heather and Welly. I . . . I understand what you feel. Remember, I was betrayed, too—by a woman."

Something flickered in the other's face. "She didn't betray me! I betrayed her. She was a friend, and I demanded more. I dragged her out of the normal comfortable world into mine. A young, kind girl, and I dragged her into the cold just to share my loneliness."

"No, Merlin, I'm sure it wasn't like. . . ."

"Oh, yes, it was. I wanted this life to be different. I wanted not to be alone. I wanted someone to love me honestly this time. And what did I do? I drove the most loving person I've ever met away from me!" The wizard stood up angrily and paced the top of the hill.

"How could I have been so blind, so egotistical as not

to know what would happen? There's nothing human left of me. I'm just an empty shell. Anything that might once have been worth loving in me was eaten up by magic long ago."

Now the king jumped to his feet. "That's not true, you crazy old man! Remember me? I'm your friend, aren't I? I've found a few lovable scraps in you."

Merlin smiled thinly. "But you're different, Arthur. You've been touched by Faerie since your birth, stubborn human that you are. But to the rest of the world, to the real world, I'm a hollow specter—useless."

"You are not useless, not unless you sit out here and let yourself starve to death! We need you, Merlin. Come on back with us. Who knows, perhaps in time there may be other. . . ."

"No!" The wizard spun around, glaring. "Never any others."

"All right, no others. I'm sorry. I'd almost forgotten how I felt about Guenevere . . . before I met Margaret." The king blushed and turned aside. "But I do need you, Merlin. And besides, you did promise us something of a prophecy."

Merlin looked down at the bowl hanging at his waist. "Yes, I did. Though whether I and this . . . this toy can still do that I just don't know. I'll try again." He sighed, rubbing a weary hand over his face. "Have some food sent out if you want. I'll try the bowl here. This is an ancient Hill of Seeing, you know."

"No, I didn't."

"You wouldn't, lucky ignorant child!" He smiled wanly. "Maybe I can't read the future, Arthur. But you do deserve a better one this time. So does our world. I'll do what I can."

Arthur laid a hand on his old friend's shoulder, then without a word turned away, beckoning Troll to follow. Once, the king turned and looked back. The thin figure on the hill seemed painfully alone.

seventeen

Exile

When Heather opened her eyes, it was to bright light and kaleidoscopic color, a dizzy riot of blue and green. She jammed her eyes shut hoping something would settle. Cautiously she opened them again, but the light and colors remained and began forming into shapes.

She was lying under a tree, a huge oak tree in full leaf. It was lit by brilliant, unfiltered sunlight, and beyond it arched bright blue sky.

Beside her, Welly's voice said, "Are we dead, do you think? Or in Avalon, maybe?"

Heather propped herself onto an elbow and looked around. This tree wasn't an isolated giant. There were others, many others, on the hillside around them. All were lushly green, touched here and there with a splash of orange or yellow. And the hillside itself was covered in grass, not coarse gray stuff but long, deep green blades. She combed her hand through them, feeling their cool softness glide between her fingers. Scattered through the grass were tiny white flowers.

Heather sighed and lay back again. "Well, it sure isn't our world. But I don't think it's Avalon either. When we were there before, it was different somehow, like this but . . . more so."

Cautiously now, Welly sat up. "Well then, where are. . . . Look at that, will you!"

Heather sat up quickly. "A city. Look at the size of that city!"

"The buildings, they're so tall!"

"And there are no ruins. Welly, do you see that?"

"I sure don't see any from here."

They both stood up. Heather turned around to where the hill rose toward the blue sky. "Let's climb up and look from there. Maybe it'll make more sense."

Scrambling up the grassy slope, they realized just how warm the air was. Both were soon sweating under the fur lining of even their light summer jackets and had to stop and strip them off. A warm breeze blew over them, in a soft unfamiliar caress.

When they reached the top, they didn't notice the view as much as the activity around them. People were everywhere on the grassy hilltop, people in bright colors and light, almost skimpy-looking clothes. And there were dogs. Heather felt her stomach tighten, remembering fell dogs. But these looked very different, both from the dogs they knew and from each other. They barked and ran about in pursuit, not of prey, but of balls and sticks people threw for them.

And children ran among them, laughing children, unafraid of dogs or anything else it seemed. Several women walked by, pushing smaller children in odd four-wheeled carriages.

A faint flapping sound came from overhead. Both instantly crouched and looked fearfully to the sky. Sunlight shone through the rainbow streamers of a kite as it dipped and soared through the air. They looked sheepishly at each other, then stood up laughing with relief. They could see now that there were other such specks in the sky, while people below tended their thin, barely visible lines.

Something else moved through the sky, something much higher. Silver glinted from outstretched wings and thunder trailed behind it. "An airplane," Welly breathed. "An ancient airplane! Great gods, Heather, where are we?"

They looked back now at the city. To the south, buildings stretched as far as they could see, their multiple windows glinting with sunlight.

"What is that?" Welly asked again.

"What is which, young man?" said a voice behind them.

They turned quickly and saw a pale old man, lightly dressed, with a little curly-haired dog on a leather strap beside him.

"Ah . . . those buildings." Welly pointed vaguely to the mysterious city.

"Well, that funny looking one there is the old Post Office Tower, and the square tower beyond it, the one with the spires, is part of the Houses of Parliament. Now over there by all those tall new buildings, you can just see the dome of St. Paul's."

Heather looked confused. "Eh, I guess we mean, what are they in general?"

"Well, those there are in Westminster, but the ones around St. Paul's are in the City."

"What city?"

"The City of London, of course."

"London!"

"From Hampstead Heath you're not thinking to see Paris, I hope?" The man seemed slightly annoyed.

"No. No, certainly not," Welly mumbled.

"Thank you," Heather squeaked out as the man and his dog, eyeing them curiously, continued their walk.

Speechless, Heather and Welly looked at each other. London. Fallen, fabled London!

"This is too incredible," Heather whispered at last. "But why did Morgan send us here? This is hardly *durance vile*."

"Maybe it's a mistake. Maybe she meant to send us back to some dinosaur swamp and ran out of oomph."

"Yeah," Heather said dreamily, then became suddenly

practical. "And she might realize her mistake any moment and blast us on again. Let's get a look at old London while we have the chance!"

Together they ran down the hill toward the distant buildings. But soon they were diverted by the natural beauty around them. Strange flowering bushes. And trees, a whole forest of them. They wandered off among the huge trunks, wondering at their height and the luxuriant greenery below.

They met other people on the paths, walking with dogs or whizzing by on alarming two-wheeled vehicles. People nodded at them in a friendly, if curious way. Even with their fleecy jackets slung over their arms and hiding their swords, they felt hot and out of place in leather trousers and heavy wool shirts.

Emerging from the trees, they entered a lane lined with houses, impressively big houses, two or three stories of brick. All of the windows were glass, and in front of each was a little walled garden brimming with flowers. The colors were dazzling in the bright sun.

Whistling with delight, Heather saw what could only be a rose, a huge pink flower with delicate open petals like she had seen in pictures. Gently she touched it, tipping it down to her face. Soft wet petals brushed her cheek, and an intoxicating aroma seemed to fill her body. She felt she could spend the rest of her life smelling that one rose.

Welly gripped her arm. Reluctantly she turned away and saw a motor-driven vehicle rumbling down the street toward them. It pulled up beside the walkway. Doors opened and two people carrying bags made of paper stepped out, then walked into one of the houses.

"Look at that car!" Welly exclaimed when they had gone. "A real ancient car. And see, there're others down the road there. Fantastic!"

He walked over to the car and cautiously ran a hand over its smooth red surface. Heather started to join him when she saw something else. On one of the garden walls an animal lay asleep in the sun. It had thick, golden fur and a long tail that drooped off the wall like a fluffy snake. As Heather watched, the creature opened one eye, gave a paw a few quick licks and rubbed this across its whiskered face.

Tentatively Heather reached out a hand. Surely this was a cat, but the only ones she had seen were the shadowy feral cats that roamed the wild lands. Those were dangerous things, silent fierce hunters. She touched the furry side, soft and warm in the sun. Lazily the cat turned its eyes toward her, then began a low contented rumbling.

"Welly, look at this! A domestic cat, and it's purring."

A woman walking by in a yellow dress smiled at her pleasantly. "Old Tom's a good cat, he is. A fine mouser, right enough, but he does like his afternoon nap."

The two children smiled self-consciously at the woman. Heather gave the cat a parting rub, then they headed down the lane, which opened into a large, noisy street. Vehicles of all descriptions roared by, and people bustled along the sidewalks. The traffic was alarming, not just the sight of it but the unfamiliar raucous noise and the hot chemical smell. The two stayed well back from the curb. Soon, however, they found that the buildings lining the sidewalk were fascinating enough.

Huge sheets of glass covered displays of things they had seen only in pictures. Some of the objects they couldn't even imagine a use for. Heather looked at the clothes and wistfully imagined herself wearing them. They were ridiculously impractical, of course—but beautiful. The two progressed slowly down the street, barely pulling themselves away from one window only to be fascinated by the next.

Outside one shop stood several tables mounded with mysterious fruits and vegetables. The aroma was enticing. For minutes Heather looked longingly at some round pinkish-yellow fruits. Her mouth was watering so hard that her cheeks hurt. Suddenly Welly appeared beside her again and dragged her to a small shop on the corner.

It's window was filled with candies, a dazzling variety. Sweet smells drifted out the door and pulled them in. Inside the cheery shop, glass counters were heaped with candies of rich brown and every possible color.

"May I help you?" a plump, white-haired lady said from behind a counter.

"Oh," Heather sighed, "they all look and smell so good. But . . . I don't know if we have any money."

"I have," Welly said, pulling a leather pouch from his pocket. Pouring several coins into his palm, he looked at them doubtfully. Two were ones Arthur had minted in Keswick, and one was Wessex coinage showing a rough profile of King Edwin.

"Will any of these do?" He handed the coins to the shop lady.

She looked them over curiously. "Foreign aren't they? But I should have guessed from your accent and clothes. Where are you from, then?"

Heather thought frantically. Geography class. What had the pre-Devastation world been like? What countries might be near Britain yet cold enough to explain their clothes? And what about their darker skin?

Welly had the answer first. "Newfoundland. We're Eskimos here on a visit."

"Eskimos. Well, fancy that. You'd better ask your hosts to give you some of our money if you're going to be visiting shops. But my grandson's a coin collector. I'll sell you some sweets for one of these with the animal on it. What is it?"

"A dragon, Ma'am."

"A dragon, how nice. Now, what would you like, duckies?"

They looked at each other helplessly, overwhelmed with indecision.

"Suppose I give you a sampling of several?" At their eager nods, she took a white paper bag and began scooping a few pieces from many piles. Finally she handed the bag to Heather, and the two remaining coins to Welly. "There you are, duckies. Enjoy your visit."

"We are," Welly said as they slipped out the door.

Outside, standing on the sidewalk, they eagerly opened the bag and went into ecstasies over every new bite. Heather particularly liked the brown ones. She wondered what they were.

"We'd better not eat them all now," she said at last. Tucking the bag into a pocket, she tried wiping the stickiness from her face, only smearing it further.

After working up courage to run across a street, they looked at shop windows in the next block. The one that most fascinated them had boxes with moving pictures behind glass sides. Some were colored pictures and some were black and white. With them went voices and music, muffled behind the shop window.

"I've read about these," Welly whispered. "Televisions. They run on electricity."

"Are those things really happening?" Heather asked.

"Somewhere. They have machines that send pictures through the air."

Several people had stopped in front of the shop now. Welly wandered down the street, but Heather stayed and watched a box showing people on tall horses riding through a beautiful countryside. They stopped in front of a big white building and several women ran out, all wearing gorgeous, colorful dresses, incredibly wide and long.

Most of those crowding around were watching one of the other boxes where a man was talking. Boring, Heather thought. Then abruptly the story stopped on her box, and a man was talking there as well. The shopkeeper reached an arm through the back and turned up the sound.

". . . about the crisis. The Prime Minister's warning was issued at 11:45 this morning. So far there has been no reply from the Soviet Union. But in Washington, the ultimatum issued by the President yesterday has spurred an emergency session of Congress. We switch now to our Washington correspondent."

Another face appeared on the screen. Heather glanced away and noticed the worried looks on the faces around her. She wished they'd show the people with horses and long dresses again. She picked another candy from the bag and began licking off the brown coating.

Suddenly Welly was tugging at her arm. "Come here. I want you to see something." His voice was strained, and he looked ghastly. Heather wondered if he'd eaten too many candies.

"Look at that!" he said when he'd dragged her down the street. In front of them was a shallow wooden stall with folded piles of printed paper on the counter.

"At what?"

"Those are newspapers. They were printed out every day. Look at the date on these."

She stepped over and examined the papers. It took her a while to find the dates above big black words like "Latest Crisis" and "New Ultimatum." She looked from one paper to another. Suddenly she understood. Fear slammed into her like a club.

"Oh no! That's the date!"

Welly nodded. "The war, the bombs, the beginning of the Devastation."

"And we're in London! The only bomb that fell in England fell here."

"Now we know why Morgan. . . ."

His words were cut off by a horrible scream. The wailing rose like a banshee's cry, filling the air with high keening.

The effect on the people around them was intense. There was a second's pause, then everyone began running somewhere. Children cried, and mothers scooped them up and ran off. Customers poured out of stores, and shopkeepers locked up immediately after them. People everywhere were yelling and screaming, car horns blared and the streets were clogged with hurrying vehicles.

In the midst of the mounting chaos, Heather and Welly stood frozen with horror. Everyone was running, but there was nowhere to run. Death was hurtling toward them, and there was no escape.

eighteen

Called to Doom

Seated on the lone hill, Merlin slowly chewed the food Troll
had brought him. He scarcely tasted it, but he knew his
neglected body needed the strength. His movements were
cool and mechanical. He felt emotionally empty and hoped
that if he could stay that way, the pain might fade.

He finished eating, then stood up, unfastening the bowl
from his belt. Deciding against using the tripod, he walked
to where bare chalk showed like bone through the grass.
Raising the gleaming bowl above his head, he turned slowly,
exposing it to all four directions. Then seating himself on
the earth, he held the bowl at eye level, tracing a thin finger
along the interweaving patterns and murmuring the invoking
spell. Setting the bowl firmly into the chalk, he took up a
waterskin and filled the bowl nearly to its snake-entwined
rim. Whispering a final phrase, he hunched over, blew on
the surface three times, and stared into the liquid. He fo-

cused his mind on the upcoming battle, on the need to see Morgan's plans.

Timelines and shadowy images swirled in the depths. Careless now of personal safety, he hurled the whole strength of his mind at the vision. But again it jiggled and sidestepped. He felt distantly the waves of power, hearing them like great music, but cracked and oddly out of tune. Briefly he caught the distorted image of a battlefield and felt a sense of place and of incredible importance. But before he could grasp even that one vision, it danced away from him and vanished in the familiar enigma, the explosion of white hate.

With a despairing cry, he smashed a hand against the bowl, staring blindly as it spun away, splashing water over the bare earth.

Clearly it was useless now—an outgrown toy, a thing hopelessly tied to the past. As was he! Was there no way he could fit into this world, to find, to understand its new strain of power? Was there even any reason for him to care any more? Torn by despair, his mind pulsed like a raw open wound.

Suddenly a new force hit it. Human need, a frightened cry for help. It sliced into him like a knife, and with it came a brief flash of understanding. Abruptly its plea was cut off by an alien blast of energy. It swept the call away and smashed into his own mind with incredible pain.

The wizard cried out and pitched forward to the ground.

Instantly the worried troll was beside him, slapping his face with cold flat hands. "Great Wizard! Not be dead. We need wizard. Troll need wizard. Please, wake up!"

Slowly Merlin began to hear and feel again, but his mind still throbbed with pain. It was minutes before he could speak even a whisper.

"Troll, I need your help."

"Anything! Wizard say, Troll obey."

He struggled to sit up, dizzily resting his head on his knees. "I felt it. Before I was attacked, I felt something new. I think, yes, I think I understand now. A little. But I must go somewhere, help someone first. It has nothing to do with

Arthur or future battles. I'm useless there. So is that old hunk of silver." He looked at the bowl lying lifeless on the grass. "Still, it did give me one thing, and it's important I pass that on. Troll, you must take a message to Arthur."

His companion looked confused. "Great Wizard be better soon, he go."

"No, I have to go elsewhere. You must tell him. Here, get me the map from the pack you brought."

The troll scuttled off. When he returned, Merlin spread the ancient paper on the ground beside him and marked a spot with a lump of chalk.

"Take this to Arthur. Tell him he must move his army southeast to that spot immediately. I don't fully know why, but it is very important that, if he is to meet Morgan's army, he do so right there. You understand all that?"

The troll nodded eagerly. "Yes, yes, Troll understand. Can tell King. But what Wizard do?"

"If I can, I'll try to join him there, though I don't know of what use I'd be. Now go on, Troll, hurry with the message. They must leave right away."

Obediently the troll trotted off, but he kept stopping and looking back, reluctant to leave the wizard. Merlin smiled encouragingly and waved until the other was out of sight. Then he sat on the ground in a weary heap.

Yet, tired as he was, a tremulous smile played over his lips. True the bowl was dead, a thing of the past. Magic tied to it had failed to bring anything but an infuriating, veiled sense of the future.

But that first blast of power, that was new. That was the new magic in all its force. And it had come to him when his mind had been torn open to human feeling, without any "thing" transmitting it—anything except the links of friendship and need. As if a curtain had finally been torn aside, Merlin began to see how this new magic must work.

Eagerly now he stood up. With that pleading cry had come a brief picture, and a fearful one—places of power, places he knew. Heather might not need his companionship, but she needed his help. He would go there.

But that would mean a hard day's ride, and time was short. There was one other way, though he hesitated to take it. It meant using a sort of magic he had never liked. And now, exhausted as he was with his fast and his efforts at *seeing*, he relished it even less. He wouldn't even be able to take his staff. But perhaps he didn't need that any more, and there really was no choice.

He stood up. The sun had already set, leaving a bloody smear against the western horizon. The evening air was cold and fresh. Breathing deeply, he looked up into the wide, beckoning sky. Like dry leaves, whispered words blew from him.

Slowly his shape began to shrink and thin. He stretched out his arms and they spread into wings. With a shrill cry he launched himself into the air.

The hawk flew off toward the sunset, the last rays rippling his feathers with gold. With powerful thrusts and long soaring glides, he sped on and on. The land below him darkened into night, but the sky was his world now. Cold wind slid beneath his wings. Smoothly he rode the wind, climbing the sudden warm gust that wafted up from the earth, that lifted him nearer to the stars. Starlight glimmered faintly on his wings, it glinted in his black eyes, it called to his mind.

His mind was a hawk's, and only with a struggle could he hold to any sense of human purpose. He had a goal and he flew there, but his thoughts were of the flight.

There were thoughts, too, of a hawk's body. He fought them, but inside the small feathered body, hunger grew. He needed food, he needed warm flesh. Slowly he dropped lower and lower to the earth, his course veering into a wide circle, sweeping back over a field. He hovered motionless in the air until there came a twitch of movement below. Like a stone he plummeted to the earth, talons extended. He heard the squeal, felt claws sink into fur and flesh. Then he was eating, beak splattered with blood, warm gobbets of meat sliding down his throat.

Refreshed, he preened his feathers, then rose into the air again. Only the tiniest corner of his mind felt revulsion.

He headed straight to the southwest. The waning moon rising behind him cast a watery light over the land below. It transformed his feathers to purest silver. The ecstasy of flight could carry him on and on.

But there was somewhere he was supposed to go, somewhere below. He cared nothing for that now; he wanted only to fly. Yet the thought dragged at him, drawing him closer to the earth.

He shifted his gaze downward to shapes that the moonlight showed sliding beneath him. There, below him now, that was what he sought. His flight circled back, echoing the shape below.

A great circle of earth and stone. The standing stones were far fewer than when his human mind had known them, the buildings more plentiful. He circled again. One ancient stone avenue was gone entirely, but another struck off to the south and east. He swooped along its course until it, too, petered out, and he glided up over a ridge. His mind's vision faded, and the strength of his small bird's body was fast failing.

He must land, touch the earth. Ahead to his right rose a tall cone-shaped hill. With weary wings he flapped toward it; no goal now but to rest. The flat summit rose toward him, and he stretched out his feet to meet it. Weakly he fluttered to the grass. Sleep blew over him before he could fold his wings.

It was the rising sun that finally roused him, brushing warmly against his eyelids, coaxing them to open. When they did, he looked at the appendage stretched out on the grass and wondered why it had no feathers.

Shivering, he remembered and sat up. He hated shape changing. Others had more of a knack for it and could slip in and out of bodies, always staying in control. It was the sort of skill Heather might well have.

Heather! It was her call that had brought him here. Here? He looked around. Yes, Silbury Hill, and before that the Avebury circle. But this surely had not been his goal, it had been. . . . His gaze wandered over the horizon, then stopped at a dark grassy scar on a ridge below. The Long Barrow!

He scrambled to his feet. His legs wobbled beneath him, and he was hungry. But his stomach churned at the memory of his last meal. Shunting the thought aside, he hurried to the edge of the hill and clambered down. The ease of flight did not even tempt him now. The earth felt wonderfully solid beneath his feet.

From the foot of the hill he struck off across fields to the barrow-topped ridge. At its base he found two horses tied to an old gate stone. Grimly he looked up and began to climb, following a faint trail in the weedy grass. Halfway up something leaped at him. Two paws slammed against his chest, two tongues licked his face.

"Rus! Down, boy. Glad to see me, are you? Where's your mistress?"

Immediately the dog calmed down. Whining, he walked slowly up the hill looking frequently over his shoulders as Merlin followed. When they reached the stones at the barrow's entrance, the dog stopped and, slinking up against Merlin's legs, began whimpering.

"I know, Rus. I have no desire to go in there either."

"And you needn't bother to, Merlin. She's not there."

Startled, he looked up. A woman stood on top of the mound gazing down at him with cool green eyes.

"Morgan," he said resignedly. Beside him, the whimpering dog pressed harder against his legs.

She laughed. "Merlin, you are so predictable, it's funny. Each time, I trap you with the same bait."

"Bait?"

"People, Merlin. Love." She walked lightly down the mound and sat on a flattened stone, swinging her legs like an innocent young girl.

"You need people, Merlin. You may spend lifetimes denying it, but you do. That's why you've never been as good a magician as I. I need only power. I feed on it, grow strong on it. But you need to love and be loved. It weakens you— to say nothing of how easy it makes you to trap."

"To trap? What do you mean? That attack might have been yours, but not that first call."

Frowning thoughtfully, the woman plucked a gorse sprig and crushed it in her hands. "No, that was hers, all right. And stronger than I expected. She does have an odd sort of power, that one. But when it comes to dealing with people, she's as weak as you are."

Laughing, she scattered gorse over the ground. The cold air turned briefly tangy with its scent. "I admit, the amulet didn't work as well on her as I had hoped. After Brecon she should have been drawn to use it until it ensnared her. She kept fighting it, even ignoring it. But then it was old and I suspect its powers had gone a little flat. It worked in the end, though."

"Amulet? What did. . . ?"

"The best part is that what finally brought her was thinking she was coming here to *save* you from dire danger. Ironic, isn't it?"

"To save me? But she . . . but the note. . . ."

"Ah yes, the note. A nice little frill of mine, don't you think? I couldn't resist. A chance to twist the knife and let you wallow in self-pity while I laid the trap."

For all his long life, Merlin had hated this woman. Suddenly, forgetting all his powers, he lunged at her like an animal. Startled, she fell back, slapping him away with a blast of power.

"Temper! Don't lose your subtlety, Merlin dear. Oh, I will miss you! This time I really must dispose of you permanently. But then there will be no one to appreciate the finesse of my powers."

Merlin had been shaking with anger, but suddenly he laughed until great gusts of laughter battered the cold evening air. "Powers? No, Morgan, your powers are nothing! They're tattered, dying relics. I've only just seen it, but surely you've feared as much. Your amulet, my bowl—they are *things*, cold, lifeless things. In this new world, trying to channel power through them is like using stone tools when iron is at hand. I don't know what you tried with that amulet, but Heather, novice that she is, was able to resist because she is part of a new power."

"You're quite mad!" Morgan's eyes flared with anger, then she leaned back and laughed derisively. "I almost hate to put you away now, because that would be a mercy. And you deserve much, much worse."

The wizard's smile was grim. "You said a moment ago that your power was greater than mine because you had no need for people. Perhaps that was true once, Morgan, but not now. The strongest new magic comes from people, not things. It comes from their hopes, their fears, their ties with each other. Your amulet worked in the end only because it used Heather's need to help . . . to help someone she cared for."

His look was pitying now. "You are still a person of power, Morgan, as am I. But keep trying to use it in the old ways, and it will prove a sterile power. You will be helpless."

"Helpless?" She jumped up, glaring at him. "In a short time your precious Arthur will see just how helpless I am! I will defeat him and his army utterly. I've worked for years, Merlin, wedging a crack in time, and through it I will call an army, an army of the dead. They will come in such numbers, reeking such despair, that Arthur's mere human army will freeze in horror, freeze while my forces seize the victory!"

He thought of his persistent vision, the twisting timeliness, the blast of white heat and hatred, then that one glimpse of a battlefield. Nothing made sense. "A crack in time? Where could you . . . ?"

"Enough, Merlin! It's been fun all these years, having an opponent almost worthy of myself. But your time is over!"

Reaching behind a stone, she pulled out a charred lump of wood. "Go join your puny friends, if they mean so much to you." She tossed him the wood. "Catch!"

Instinctively he did. It was like clamping down on an explosive. His self shattered apart, its shreds spinning over an immensity of collapsing time.

Like a leaf, he was swept down an endless dark stream. Eternity flowed past. Then he seemed to be caught by a web of roots, washed up against the base of a great tree.

Slowly the world stopped rocking beneath him. He felt the softness of grass, the solidity of earth. The air was gentle and warm. He opened his eyes. A massive oak tree spread above him. Beyond it was bright blue sky.

Dizzily he sat up. Beside him, Rus crouched on the grass, both faces looking bewildered. From behind them, a shrill barking shattered the air. Quickly Merlin looked around to see a small curly-haired dog yapping and straining at a leash. On its other end, a pale old man was holding him back and looking thoroughly aghast at the sight of Rus.

"Oh." Hastily Merlin waved a hand over the mutant dog. One head and one tail became invisible.

Startled, the old man now shifted his gaze to Merlin and his fur-lined clothing. Then he yanked his dog away and went off muttering, "More of those crazy kids. What is the world coming to?"

Unsteadily Merlin got to his feet, looking around in vague recognition. Their world somewhere in the past. Then he glanced down at Rus and laughed. The visible head and tail were off-set, leaving room for their invisible companions.

"Come on, you lopsided mutt, we've got to find Heather and Welly. Go on, find your mistress."

Excitedly the dog jumped about; then smelling the ground, he suddenly shot off down the hill. Fur coat flying and sword banging against his leg, Merlin raced after him.

They ran over the grass then cut to the right following winding paths among a forest of trees. Merlin wanted to stop and look around, but more than that he wanted to see Heather. She hadn't written that note! She'd wanted to help him, not leave him! He paid no attention to the startled looks that swept them as they raced past.

Rus slowed when they came out onto a lane. His long nails clicked on the unfamiliar pavement. Nose down, he moved steadily along. A startled yellow cat bristled at him from atop a wall, but the dog spared it only a passing snarl.

The noise of traffic grew until they reached a large busy street.

Suddenly a distant wailing rose and filled the air. Rus sat back and howled with both throats, visible and invisible. Puzzled, Merlin looked about. Then he caught something of the fear and urgency around them.

"Go on, Rus, find them. Hurry!"

The dog took off down the sidewalk, and Merlin followed, dodging around rushing, panicky people. They crossed another street, and then he saw them. Standing like an island in a sea of chaos, Heather and Welly huddled together against a building, fear and hopelessness written on their faces.

Rushing madly toward them, Merlin grabbed Heather in his arms and kissed her on her chocolate-smeared mouth.

Welly looked on in happy surprise. "Well, it's about time you did that." Suddenly he sobered. "But it's not the right time—the world's about to blow up!"

Merlin looked at him, confused.

"The Devastation!" the boy yelled over the noise of people and sirens. "Morgan sent us back to the day it began!"

"And this is London!" Heather added, clutching his arm.

Realization dawned on Merlin. "Of course, a way to really destroy me." His look of horror slid into excitement. "But no . . . the crack in time. Her 'army of the dead.' From here, of course! It will still be open for them. Heather, the new power, the new magic, if we can use it. . . . Hurry, back to the tree! The opening must be there."

"How?" Welly protested. "We don't know where. . . ."

"Rus does. Follow him!"

Crazily the three pelted after the dog. Everyone else, intent on their own panic, ignored them. Sirens wailed on and on throughout the vast city. The park was nearly deserted as they ran gasping up the hill.

Suddenly Heather slowed. Looking up, she scanned the blue sky. A graceful white gull soared overhead.

"Earl! The vision I saw. I just realized. . . . This is the City! Look, there's the bird!"

He turned back and grabbed her arm. "Of course, yes.

Your vision." He pulled her after him. "Then use it, Heather! Use the new power. Focus through that bird, the dog, the tree, through every living thing around it."

"But you . . . you haven't your staff."

"But I have you!" His smile shone. "I'll focus through you and Welly . . . and through Arthur. Arthur back there needs us desperately. Now, quick, grab Welly's hand. Welly, hold Rus."

They flung themselves against the rough bark of the tree. As Merlin chanted phrases beside her, she felt the touch of his love and his power, new and strong as she had never felt it before. Reaching into new depths of her own, she let her power rise through her, stretching out to the others, binding them in strength and need. Visions of their time, their king, and each other formed in their minds.

Suddenly behind them the sirens stopped. All sound stopped. A blinding whiteness filled the world, and a searing heat. Its horrible power slammed behind theirs, as they hurtled through time.

nineteen

To the Ends of the Earth

The army led by Arthur Pendragon was nearing its goal. It had not been an easy matter, arriving where they were. The order to abandon their strategic position had been hard for some of the allied leaders to accept, particularly on the word of a demented boy wizard brought by a scuttling one-eared troll.

But to Arthur's surprise, Margaret of the Scots had been his staunchest supporter. "If that skinny kid says we must do something," the queen had said, "and Arthur believes him, then we must do it. This King Arthur of ours has led us through a good many improbable situations already. I, for one, am ready to follow him to the ends of the earth."

Arthur treasured that statement and what it reflected. In the end, the others had agreed with her. And now, shadowed by forces out of Faerie, they followed behind him toward the site of ancient London. But as they rode on, their route became more and more daunting.

At first there were the usual abandoned buildings. Then there were ruins that seemed to come from more than neglect, empty stone shells and buildings that lifted only twisted metal skeletons to the sky. Finally there were no ruins at all, only an empty glassy plain. Ghosts of snow twisted and whispered dryly across its surface.

Londinium, Arthur thought sadly. A sleepy little town on the River Thames, then later, it seemed, the capital of a great nation. If there was anything left of even that river now, it was the faint dry scar that seamed the desolate plain below them. On a hollow wind, snow blew across the wasteland like drifting sand.

It was almost with relief that they saw Morgan's army approaching. Any life and promise of action was better than this. The enemy poured over the plain in a black wave, while the armies of the West and North watched and felt relief turn into growing uneasiness.

Arthur squinted against the glare of snow and patches of mirror-like earth. Of the human warriors marching toward them, most, he imagined, were not volunteers. Once Morgan's forces won a land, the locals had little choice but to do her bidding. But it was the other soldiers who were more worrisome. There were mutants from beyond the channel, and most chilling of all were the allies from beyond this world. Arthur had never seen their like in such numbers. For his own army, bred in a different age, he knew this must be unimagined nightmare.

He looked to his right, smiling encouragement at Margaret. Grimly she returned his smile, her face unusually pale against her crown of red hair. Sighing to himself, Arthur wished that Merlin rode at his other side. It wasn't the magic he needed so much as the well-tested companionship and counsel. But he could spare little time at present to wonder about his friend. A battle lay at hand, a decisive battle. The king needed no prophecy to see that.

As the enemy neared, one rider came forward, halting on a bare rise. Black hair blew about her shoulders, and her restive mount hissed and pawed the hard earth with its claws.

The woman's voice rang powerfully over the shifting silence.

"Arthur Pendragon. After two thousand years, we meet again. It was very thoughtful of you to come this far to meet me, but hardly necessary. You could have lost this battle just as well where you were."

"I have no intention of losing this time, Morgan."

"But you will, just the same. Your army is large, but it can never equal mine. You haven't even your pathetic little wizard with you. Of course, you are right, you need not lose. You could join with me. We could conquer the rest of this wretched world together. Think of it, you as High King again, and I as your queen. You don't need that red-haired Scottish harpy any longer."

Beside him, Queen Margaret snarled and hurled her war spear toward the enemy. Arthur laughed heartily. "This is a queen after my own heart. You have your answer, Morgan." He turned in his saddle. "Sound the charge!"

Trumpets, horses, and the battle cries of men and nonmen—the sound of warfare broke out on the long-dead and silent plain.

But Morgan did not engage in the fighting. Instead, she clothed herself in flame and power and worked a terrible invocation. Dragging forth power long prepared, she reached back into time, to a day of empty horror, to a day when this plain was peopled neither with warriors nor with city dwellers, but with the restless spirits of countless newly dead. She called forth these spirits. Held by power and their own aimless misery, they came.

Amid Arthur's army a gray cloud began to swirl. It formed into shapes hardly more solid than mist. Images of death—creatures seared into ashes, vaporized into shadows on a wall. Into the midst of living warriors came specters whose skin hung off them in rags, whose bodies were blistered like scorched meat, whose hollow eyes ran with blood.

They floated by in anguished, unspeaking torment, and the living around them went mad with fear. Brave warriors threw down their weapons and ran. Horses twisted under their riders and stampeded off. Even among those from

Faerie, many quailed and slipped away like smoke.

Those around Arthur tried to hold their ground, but fear rose in a choking cloud, gripping both horses and riders. Some closed their eyes and huddled together. Squealing, Troll rolled on the ground, throwing hairy arms over his head.

Suddenly there was a deafening crack, as if the world had split open. Three young people and a dog stood before them, beside a stump of charred wood. Overhead, a black crow screamed and flew off over a plain that was littered with fear-stunned bodies.

Merlin leaped forward. Above the moaning and wailing he shouted, "Morgan, go! You are defeated! The spirits of people can not be an enemy now. It is *things* we fight against!" Chanting, he thrust his arms into the air. "By the power of human pity, I send these spirits back to their rest!"

The gray shapes churned and thinned like wind-blown smoke. Morgan shrieked in fury, then cried out, "You cannot win, Merlin! In the end, your side will lose as it has before."

"Perhaps, but I think not. The world has changed, Morgan. And now I would have it change more!"

Turning, he strode back to the tree stump. "You opened a crack, Morgan La Fay. Now, I call through it other things. I call the picture of our real enemy, a vision of soulless things gone mad. May its image burn into every soul here and, through them, onto the furthest generation! And I call, too, the human cry of its victims. May its echoes haunt mankind for all eternity!" He stomped a foot down on the charred wood.

It seemed that heat filled the plain, as if a giant oven had been flung open. There came a concussion of sound like the scream of dying suns, and with it millions of screams from severed lives. Blinding light burst upon them, searing into the very cells of their bodies. The memory of what had been, and what could be again, sealed there forever.

A cold wind of their own world revived them at last. People staggered to their feet, all military order gone. Morgan had fled, and her followers, shaken and abandoned, were slinking away.

The soldiers of the West and North, seeing their leaders still among them, rallied to the Lion and Dragon banners snapping in the cold, clean wind. All were subdued and quiet.

Arthur Pendragon surveyed the field, then turned to his oldest friend. "Even as a vision, that weapon and its effects. . . ." He broke off, struggling to control a new wave of shuddering. Then grimly he smiled at Merlin. "But, still, you saved us, old wizard. Now, will you finally prophesy for us? Is Morgan gone for good? By what you have done, will we finally live in peace?"

Merlin put a hand on the king's shoulder. "Arthur, you were always a dreamer. No, Morgan or others like her will surely be back. And as for peace . . . we are dealing with human beings, creatures that fight among themselves and want what the other has. Changing that will not be easy. Though with this new sort of power, there may be some hope."

The wizard looked at the crowd growing around them. He grinned at Troll's bouncy greeting, then jumped onto the old charred stump. "But here I will prophesy. The nature of humankind may linger, but the memory of this ultimate horror will be carried with each of us as well. By the new powers, it is sealed in every one of the thousands who were here today, friend and foe alike. Their descendants will carry it in their bodies and spread it, a racial memory to pass on for all time.

"Perhaps people will still fight and make weapons, but this one scorching memory may turn them back from that final horror. They may gallop wildly down the same road, but now, perhaps, they will turn aside before the precipice. And, Arthur, perhaps this time you and your queen can lay foundations for a world that will not topple. There is strong, new, human power in today's magic. We can use it to build a world of hope.

"There! You wanted prophecy, and you have it!" Laughing, the wizard spun around and pointed at Kyle the harper. "Now make that into a song if you will, a song to ring through time. But don't forget the verse about how this world's sorcerers—and sorceresses—are human, too, and will be part of the new world as well!"

Hesitantly, he reached out a hand to Heather. Running to him, she threw her arms around his neck and kissed him joyfully. Then she drew back.

"Earl Bedwas, I thought so! Or perhaps I should start calling you Aged Merlin."

"Huh?"

"It's just that I do believe you are finally growing a beard!"

Startled, he raised a hand to his slightly scratchy chin. "Well, it's about time!"

Lincoln High School Library

DATE		
NO 23 '88	OC 12 92	
JA 31 '89		
AP 6 '89	OC 26 '92	
NO 27 '89	JA 4 '93	
JA 29 '90	FEB 04 05	
FE 12 '90	OCT 2 2 '07	
OC 17 '90		
OC 31 '90		
AP 18 '91		

A665

© THE BAKER & TAYLOR CO.